D0313263

Charmseekers

Books 7 – 9

Amy Tree

Illustrated by Gwen Millward

Orion
Children's Books

First published in Great Britain in 2010
by Orion Children's Books
a division of the Orion Publishing Group Ltd
Orion House
5 Upper St Martin's Lane
London WC2H 9EA

An Hachette UK Company

1 3 5 7 9 8 6 4 2

A catalogue record for this book is available from the British Library.

ISBN 978 1 4440 0132 7

Printed and bound in the UK by
CPI Mackays, Chatham ME5 8TD

www.orionbooks.co.uk
www.charmseekers.co.uk

CONTENTS

The Thirteen Charms of Karisma

When Charm became queen of Karisma, the wise and beautiful Silversmith made her a precious gift. It was a bracelet. On it were fastened thirteen silver amulets, which the Silversmith called 'charms', in honour of the new queen.

It was part of Karisma law. Whenever there was a new ruler, the Silversmith made a special gift, to help them care for the world they had inherited. And this time it was a bracelet. She told Queen Charm it was magical because the charms held the power to control the forces of nature and keep everything in balance. She must take the greatest care of them. As long as she, and she alone, had possession of the charms, all would be well.

And so it was, until the bracelet was stolen by a spider, and fell into the hands of Zorgan, the magician. Then there was chaos!

The Magic Crystals

For Imogen and Neil — with love

KARISMA

CAPE CAT

CLOVER FIELDS

HEARTMOOR

DOLPHIN BAY

MOUNT TUNA

The Silver Pool

KEY POINT

SWAMPS

JUNGLE

MERMAID ROCK

BUTTERFLY BAY

One

Sesame Brown woke one morning, threw off her duvet and jumped out of bed. When she looked out of the window, her big brown eyes opened wide with surprise. It was snowing! Thick, white snowflakes spiralled down and settled on trees, rooftops and hedges. They piled up and covered everything in a glistening eiderdown of dazzling brilliance.

"Yippee!" cried Sesame, grabbing her teddy, Alfie, and dancing round the room. "Snow, snow, snow!" she sang happily, at the top of her voice.

Her dad looked round the door.

"You're bonkers!" said Nic, and laughed. "Come down for breakfast, Ses. We're going to the park. I want to take some pictures—"

"Ooo! Can I try out my toboggan, Dad?" asked Sesame. "Can I ask Maddy to come? *Please*."

"Fine," said Nic. "We'll pick Maddy up on the way. Say about ten? But we can't stay too long. I must send some pix by lunchtime."

Nic Brown was a press photographer for THE DAILY TIMES, so Sesame was used to him always being in a rush to meet deadlines. Nic went downstairs to make coffee, leaving Sesame to get ready. She checked the time on her smart new watch (a Christmas present from her dad) then quickly texted Maddy:

Maddy replied almost immediately:

HI! CAN U CUM SLEDGING IN THE PARK? WE WILL PICK U UP AT 10. MWAH MWAH SES :)

KL! MUM SAYS YES. CNT W8. CU L8R LOL MADDY XX :) :)

16

After breakfast,
Sesame pulled on a pair of
fur-lined boots, zipped up the warm jacket
her gran had given her and wound a pink and pale
green stripy scarf round her neck. It was a present
from her riding teacher, Jodie Luck. Sesame thought
Jodie must have chosen the scarf with care, because
it was just her style! For a moment she stood
thinking about her dad and Jodie, who had been
seeing quite a lot of each other during the
Christmas holidays. They seemed very happy
together. She was pleased for her dad and had grown

to like Jodie, more and more . . . A shout from Nic at the foot of the stairs roused Sesame from her daydream:

"Hurry up, Ses! I'll wait for you in the car."

"Down in five!" she promised.

Hastily, she rummaged in a drawer for a pair of purple mittens and earmuffs, then looked in the mirror.

"Oh, no," she said. "I've forgotten my necklace." It was her favourite, a silver chain and locket, with pictures of her parents inside. It was in its usual place on her beside table, lying next to her special jewellery box.

The box where she had put (for safekeeping) the bracelet and six silver charms belonging to Queen Charm. Sesame was anxious about the seven charms still missing. "I hope I go back to Karisma soon," she said aloud, as she put her necklace on. "I *must* find all the charms!" The clasp closed with a reassuring *click*, but Sesame checked it again to be sure it was securely fastened. I don't want to lose my locket in the snow, she thought, as she hurried downstairs to pick up her toboggan.

Outside it was unusually quiet and still. Sesame liked the sound of the snow crunching beneath her boots as she made her way to the car. *Crunch, crunch, crunch!* She smiled at Chips and Pins, who were gingerly stepping across the snow-covered lawn, leaving trails of tiny paw prints, and when some snowflakes settled on her eyelashes she brushed them away, laughing.

"Dad," she said, climbing into the back of the car and fastening her seatbelt. "Did you know that every snowflake is different? We did this project at school and Mrs Wilks told us that no two snowflakes are exactly alike."

"How does Mrs Wilks know?" said Nic, starting the engine. "Don't tell me she's checked them all!"

Sesame rolled her eyes.

"D-A-D! It's true."

Maddy Webb lived on the other side of town. Sesame often wished her best friend lived closer, because they did absolutely everything together. When Nic pulled up outside her house just before ten,

Maddy was already waiting for them on the doorstep. She kissed her mum goodbye, then trudged through snow to the car.

"You look gorge!" said Sesame, admiring Maddy's ice-blue top and hood, trimmed with fun-fur.

"Thanks," said Maddy, striking a pose like a fashion model. "Present from Mum. Oh, I love your scarf—"

"Come on," said Nic. "Or the snow will melt. Once you two start talking about clothes, you never stop!"

"*Wheeeeeeee!*" yelled Sesame and Maddy, whizzing down a slippery slope for the umpteenth time. They landed with a *bump* at Nic's feet.

"Time to go," he said, glancing at his watch. "I've got some great shots of people skating. The lake's completely frozen. I must send them to the picture editor—"

"Just *one* more go, Dad," implored Sesame.

"S-e-s—"

"*PLEASE!*"

"Okay," said Nic, half-distracted selecting pictures on his digital camera and resetting the lens

to zoom. "Once more. I'll take your picture as you come down."

Sesame hugged him and scrambled up the slope after Maddy. The girls positioned the toboggan so they could get a good clear run, with Sesame sitting in front and Maddy behind.

"Ready?" said Sesame.

Maddy wrapped her arms around Sesame's waist.

"Let's go!"

The toboggan slid over the glassy surface, faster than ever. The girls shrieked with the thrill of the speed, the wind whistling in their ears and snow-spray stinging their cheeks. Faster and faster they flew, until *crump!* They landed in a snowdrift, which had mysteriously appeared from nowhere. It exploded into a million crystals that sparkled like diamonds in the sun. To their surprise, the snow didn't feel wet or cold – it was more like falling into a cloud of cotton wool. Sesame felt her necklace tingle and next thing she knew, she and Maddy were whirling around in a flurry of snowflakes. Sesame gasped. She was sure, without the shadow of a doubt, they were on their way to Karisma.

"Maddy!" she heard herself cry as she tumbled head-over-heels through the snow.

"S-e-s-a-m-e!" came Maddy's tiny voice from far away.

The Charmseekers were off on another adventure, to search for the missing charms!

Two

Nix had failed in her mission to snatch Sesame's locket. The pixie had tried, but Sesame had got away in a magic balloon with three of her friends. When Nix returned to Zorgan empty-handed, the magician had been furious . . .

"Useless magwort!* I programmed you to carry out my orders, not to FAIL!"

"I'm sorry Master. I did my best—"

* *

* **Magwort** — probably the worst name you could call anyone!

24

"Well, your best wasn't good enough, you idle doofer!* You shall be punished. Go to my library and dust ALL my books. There are five-thousand-six-hundred-and-ninety-nine. Ha! That should teach you a lesson. Get busy and don't stop till you've finished . . ."

✦ ✦ ✦

And Nix had been dusting ever since.

Now, as Zorgan looked from his Star Room at the top of his tower, his attention turned back to Charm's bracelet. His head swam with visions of what he would do once he had control of the magical charms. Morbrecia would have to become queen and wear the bracelet, because the Silversmith had made very sure it wouldn't work for him!

* *
Doofer — idiot of the first order. Brainless

Thoughtfully he rubbed the sore place on his wrist, where the charm bracelet had once burned him.

"Once Morbrecia has the bracelet, I'll empower it with Dark Magic. Then *I* shall be in control of its forces!"

Zorgan shook his head and stroked his pet bandrall,* Vanda.

* * * * * * * * * * * *
✷ Bandrall – rare flying mammal, native to Karisma

"Enough daydreaming!" he muttered. "It's time to plan my next move. Hushish!* So much depends on my taking possession of Sesame Brown's special locket. I must hold it, to put her under my spell. Then the Silversmith will lose contact with her special Seeker and Sesame will bring *me* the charms! Hm! I *wish* I knew where she's hiding the ones she's found. I've no doubt she'll be back to look for the others. And when she is, I'll be waiting for her!"

* *
*Hushish — a word used to express dismay

Three

The icehouse was amazing. After falling through a silvery mist, the girls landed in a vast hall where the glassy floors and walls were made entirely of blue-green ice. In the middle was a dome, with thirteen numbers and words carved around its base.

"Wow!" said Sesame. "Where are we?"

"In a jolly cold place," said Maddy. "Oh, who's that?"

Sesame turned to see a young woman gliding towards them. She was wearing a dress spun from fine, frosty threads, which sparkled like tinsel on a Christmas tree. She looked beautiful, but Sesame thought she must be sad because what appeared to be tears were trickling down her lovely cheeks.

"I think she's crying!" she whispered to Maddy. To her embarrassment, her words echoed round the hall. *S-H-E -'S C-R-Y-I-N-G C-R-Y-I-N-G C-R-Y-I-N-G!*

"I'm not crying," said the woman. "I'm melting!"

"I'm sorry," said Sesame. "I didn't mean to be rude."

"Gosh," said Maddy. "How awful."

The girls introduced themselves, and the woman knew at once they were Charmseekers. "Fairday, welcome to the Ice Country!" she said. "I'm Gatekeeper Seven. I'm known as the Ice Maiden. But if I go on melting . . . "

"But why *are* you melting?" asked Sesame.

"Things started to go wrong the day Queen Charm's bracelet was stolen," said the Ice Maiden, wiping a drop of water from her chin. "Since the thirteen silver charms were lost, the climate has changed and now I'm much too warm."

"It's weird," said Maddy, watching her breath make little clouds of vapour. "It feels cold as a freezer to me."

* * * * * * * * * * * * * *

*Fairday – a typical Karisman friendly greeting

29

"Yes, I expect it does," said the Ice Maiden. "But even a small rise in temperature makes a difference to us here. It's a slow business but it's happening all the same. Take my friend Karvig, the Snow Bear. He is suffering, poor thing, because the ice is melting and his habitat is being destroyed. He has to go further and further from his cave to hunt for food. Karvig *hates* warm weather!"

"I think something similar is happening in our world," said Sesame. "I read about Polar Bears in my *Wild About Wildlife* magazine. They're an endangered species!"

"I'm very sorry to hear it," said the Ice Maiden, as yet another tear trickled down her cheek. "On Karisma, the thirteen magical charms helped to control the forces of nature. *Together* they kept everything in balance. Since they've been lost, it's been chaos—" She broke off suddenly and shook her head. "Silly me! Why am I telling you this? You're Charmseekers! You must know all about the charms."

"We know the charms are special," said Sesame. "But we had no idea *why* it was so important for them to be together."

"We've found six!" said Maddy.

"They're safe in my jewellery box at home," explained Sesame. "Seven charms are still missing. We *must* find them!"

"Which ones are they?" asked the Ice Maiden.

Maddy remembered four:

"The coin, star, dolphin and cloverleaf—"

"Moon, key and . . . snowflake," said Sesame, pausing for a split-second before saying the last one. An interesting idea had dawned on her. "We're in the Ice Country, right? It's possible we might find the snowflake charm here."

"You may be right," said the Ice Maiden, with a smile. "Keep your ears and eyes open for clues."

"I will," said Sesame, excited at the prospect of finding another charm. "Sesame Brown will track it down! I can't wait to get started. What time do we have to be back?"

"By the Meeting of the Moons," said the gatekeeper.

"This is the mede of Nerox, the seventh mede in our calendar. It's the time of year when the two moons of Karisma pass each other in a total eclipse. And today is the day!"

While the gatekeeper had been talking, Maddy had noticed the word 'Nerox' carved at the base of the dome.

* *

✷ Mede — month

31

It was one of the words they'd spotted earlier; she guessed the other twelve were medes too, because there was a verse written on the walls:

A TIME FOR WINTER, ICE AND SNOW,
A TIME FOR SPRING AND CROPS TO GROW.
A TIME FOR SUMMER'S RIPENING SUN —
A TIME FOR AUTUMN, BEFORE THE YEAR IS DONE

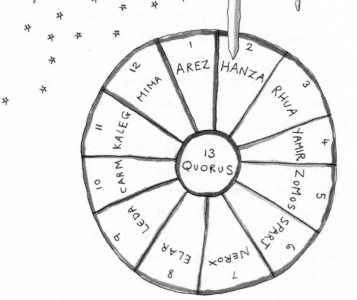

Meanwhile, Sesame could see a puddle of water forming at the Ice Maiden's feet. It was clear she was melting fast! Sesame *SO* wanted to help the gatekeeper, but how? Even if they found all the missing charms at once, she reasoned, it would probably be too late to save her. It seemed hopeless.

"Is there anything we can do to help you?" she asked.

The Ice Maiden sighed. There *was* something, but she knew it would mean placing the Charmseekers in great danger.

"Anything?" prompted Maddy, catching Sesame's worried expression.

"Well," said the Ice Maiden. "There are three crystals that are so cold they will stop me melting. I'm afraid their magic is not powerful enough to save the Ice Country. Only the precious charms can do that. But the crystals would help me."

"Where are they?" asked Sesame.

"In a grotto, deep inside a mountain," said the Ice Maiden. "But if you touch the wrong ones, you'll turn into pillars of ice!"

Four

The Silversmith paced the floor of her workshop, thinking. Thinking! She passed the thirteen magic candles; seven burn brightly for their missing charms, and her thoughts turned to her Seeker. She can't explain it, but her mystic powers tell her that Sesame is not so far away. And she's not alone. She and her friend are in a very cold place.

"Ah!" she said to herself, tossing back her long, silver hair. "I think Sesame may be in our beautiful Ice Country." Quicksilver thoughts darted like fireflies through her head, and she held in her mind the image of the magicial snowflake charm. It was a long time ago when she had made the perfect silver snowflake and the other twelve charms, here in her workshop. And now she sensed the lost snowflake charm was somewhere icy cold . . .

Suddenly her thoughts were shattered by the vision of Zorgan – bursting into her head like a bad dream.

"Tell me where Sesame has taken the charms. I know they're somewhere in the Outworld.* Supposing your special Seeker plans to keep them for herself? Then what? Tell me what I need to know, Silversmith. We could help each other . . ."

"No! Never! I know you're planning something, Zorgan. Your sinister schemes fill my mind like a nightmare. Balam** magician! If you dare harm Sesame. If you put her under a spell . . ."

"Curses on you, Silversmith. You'll regret you trusted Sesame Brown. You'll see!"

* **Outworld** – the name Karismans call our world
** **Balam** – cursed or damned

The terrifying image of Zorgan vanished, and the Silversmith breathed a sigh of relief. "Two can play at mind games, Zorgan," she said. "And this time I've proved the better player!"

But she knew Zorgan wouldn't give up.

Five

"Fantastic!" shouted Sesame.

"Totally brill!" yelled Maddy.

The Charmseekers were sitting side by side in a sleigh, going at a terrific speed across dazzling white snowfields. The sleigh belonged to the Ice Maiden, and was being drawn by a pretty dappled-grey pony called Frosty. She reminded Sesame of her favourite pony, Silver, at Jodie's riding stables.

"Frosty will take you as far as the crevasse," the Ice Maiden had told them. "From there you must continue on foot to the Snowflake Mountains."

Maddy was clutching a small glass casket the gatekeeper had given her. "To put the crystals in," she had said.

For a while the girls sat back and enjoyed their dash through the winter wonderland of the Ice Country. They felt exhilarated, skimming along through plumes of snow, while over their heads an amazing display of trembling lights danced in the sky. It was a breathtaking sight.

"Wow!" exclaimed Sesame, as swathes of incandescent orange, pink and green folds swept the sky, like shimmering curtains of light.

"It's an aurora," said Maddy.

"I saw a TV programme once about the Northern Lights. They looked like this."

All too soon their sleigh ride came to an end. Frosty stopped by a narrow ice bridge, which crossed a crevasse, and the girls got out. They patted the pony and thanked her, before she turned for home.

Sesame went to the edge of the crevasse and peered over. She gasped in horror.

"It's VERY deep! I can't see the bottom."

"Ooo!" moaned Maddy. "I feel dizzy. Do we *have* to cross it?"

On the far side the girls could see the Snowflake Mountains, and on the near side the snowfields stretched away in the distance.

In between lay the chasm, with no other crossing place in sight.

"There's no other way," said Sesame. "We *have* to get to the mountains. The grotto is there somewhere. Follow me. You'll be okay."

It was terrifying.

The ice bridge was slippery.

The frozen layers were covered with a sugaring of crisp snow, and there was nothing to prevent the girls falling into the yawning ravine below. Slowly, Sesame put one foot in front of the other, testing the firmness of the ice with every step. *Crunch, crunch, crunch!* What if it breaks? she thought. No! *Don't* think. Just keep going! Maddy was close behind. Every now and then Sesame heard her whimper, and knew how frightened she must be.

"We're nearly there," she said. "Don't look down. You're doing brilliantly. Only a few more steps—"

"Aaaaaagh!"

Both girls shrieked in terror. Sesame had slipped and was lying flat on her back – one leg dangling over the drop. One wrong move, and I'm gone! she thought.

"D-d-don't m-m-m-move," said Maddy. "I'm c-c-c-coming."

She went down on her hands and knees and crawled towards Sesame, her fear of heights suddenly forgotten. Rescuing Sesame was all she could think about.

"Give me your hand," said Maddy. "I'll pull you away from the edge."

"I'm scared I'll fall," wailed Sesame. "I'm slipping—"

"Hand," said Maddy. "Now!"

Just in time, Sesame shot out her arm and Maddy grabbed her by the wrist; then she heaved with all her strength and pulled Sesame to safety.

"Phew!" said Sesame. "That was close. Thanks, Maddy. You were awesome!"

After the drama of crossing the crevasse the girls felt a bit shaky, but they hurried on to the Snowflake Mountains. Before long they reached the foothills and found themselves walking through a pine forest, where the branches were decked with snow. The air was very still. Once or twice they thought they felt a vibration along the forest floor – as if something very big was moving about.

"Spooky!" Maddy said. She still felt a bit trembly after the crevasse.

A moment later Sesame's sharp eyes spotted a paw mark in the snow, then another and another. They were huge – about the size of dinner plates! She nudged Maddy, and together they picked out a trail of paw prints, winding through the trees.

"Let's follow them," said Sesame. "You never know, they might lead us to the charm or the grotto—"

"Or a grizzly beast with fangs!" said Maddy.

"True," she said. "But it's a risk we've got to take. I've got a feeling we'll be lucky. Remember the Ice Maiden told us to keep our ears and eyes open for clues? Well, I reckon this is one of them."

Maddy knew it was useless to argue. Once Sesame had made up her mind to do something, there was no holding her back!

45

Six

The cave was covered in a mantle of ice and icicles hung from its mouth, like long, pointed teeth. For some time the Charmseekers followed the trail of paw prints, which eventually led them to a large cave. Now they saw a fresh track of prints leading away from the cave, and Sesame was sure that whatever had made them had recently gone out.

"*Please* be careful, Ses!" said Maddy, as she watched her disappear inside.

"It's empty," said Sesame. "Oh, Maddy. Come and see!"

As she entered the cave, Maddy ducked to avoid a needle-sharp icicle and found Sesame standing next to some fantastic ice formations, rising from the rocky floor, like strange sculptures.

"Funky!" she exclaimed.

Beneath her jacket, Sesame felt her necklace warm against her neck – it was unusually warm and tingling! Her tummy flipped. Was it another clue?

Maybe the snowflake charm was here! No, there was something else. A voice. She could hear an eerie voice inside her head and it sounded familiar.

"Pillars of ice! Pillars of ice!"

"What's up, Ses?" asked Maddy, breaking into her thoughts. "You've got one of your funny looks."

"Weird," said Sesame, shaking her head. "I thought I was on to something. I was convinced we'd find the snowflake charm here, but maybe . . ."

Her words trailed off, leaving Maddy bemused.

"What *are* you babbling about?" she said.

"Sorry," said Sesame. "I heard someone saying 'pillars of ice' and I thought—"

"*That's* what the gatekeeper said we'd turn into if we touched the wrong crystals!" said Maddy.

"Of course!" said Sesame. "It must have been a warning."

The girls tried to imagine what it would be like to be frozen forever as columns of solid ice, and shuddered at the thought. Was this what fate had in store for them?

"Come on," said Sesame, hastily brushing the horrid thoughts aside. "There's no point hanging around here.

47

We must look for the charm and those three crystals!"

"*And* be back by the Meeting of the Moons," added Maddy. "How will we know when that is?"

Instinctively Sesame glanced at her cool new watch, and was not surprised to see that the dial had changed. The digital display had been replaced with an image of two moons, drifting across a starry sky. They appeared to be gradually moving closer together, just as the Ice Maiden had described.

"I reckon they're about halfway to the eclipse," she said.

"Right," said Maddy. "Let's get going!"

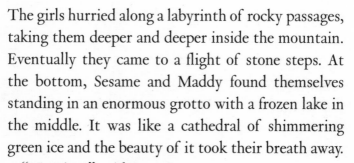

The girls hurried along a labyrinth of rocky passages, taking them deeper and deeper inside the mountain. Eventually they came to a flight of stone steps. At the bottom, Sesame and Maddy found themselves standing in an enormous grotto with a frozen lake in the middle. It was like a cathedral of shimmering green ice and the beauty of it took their breath away.

"Amazing!" said Sesame.

"Fabulous!" said Maddy.

Awestruck, they gazed upwards. A large number of stalactites hung from the roof, and below each one dangled a sparkling crystal.

"Oh!" sighed Maddy. "It's like a beautiful chandelier."

Sesame nodded. She loved the way the crystals seemed to dance, their rainbow colours gleaming with every twist and twirl.

"Let's take a closer look," she said. "We may find the magic crystals the Ice Maiden needs here."

They slid across the lake until they were standing just below the chandelier. Curiously Sesame and Maddy found they could reach the crystals easily — although they didn't dare touch them. They didn't need reminding of their fate, if they should choose the wrong ones!

"How are we supposed to know which are the crystals we need?" said Maddy. "The Ice Maiden didn't say. They all look the same to me."

But Sesame had been examining them more closely.

"No, they're different," she said. "There's a star, a round one, a triangle, a diamond and—"

"You're right!" said Maddy. "They *are* different. But how does that help us pick the right crystals?"

"Hm," said Sesame. "Let me think. They're special, right?"

Maddy nodded and Sesame continued with her theory:

"I reckon they'll be different to all the others. They'll have a *special* shape of their own!"

"Cool," said Maddy. "So, if you're right, we're looking for three crystals with the *same* shape but not like any of the others?"

"Got it in one!" said Sesame.

They searched and searched among the sparkling crystals, until Sesame gave an excited squeal.

"Here's a different one, Maddy," she said. "Look, it's got six sides and it's much brighter than the others. It *must* be a magic crystal!"

"Ooo," said Maddy. "You could be right."

"Only one way to find out—" said Sesame.

"Wait!" said Maddy, panicking. The gatekeeper's dire warning was ringing in her ears, and she was afraid Sesame would turn into a block of ice.

Maddy had never felt so helpless. She gave Sesame their Charmseekers hand sign, for luck.

"Thanks," said Sesame, returning the sign. She felt nervous too, but she wanted to reassure Maddy by trying to look and sound confident. "Here goes!"

She reached up to touch the crystal . . .

"Yesss!" cried Sesame triumphantly, when for an instant, she held the freezing crystal. It glowed with a blue light but it was SO cold, it burned her fingers.

"Here," said Maddy, quickly opening the small glass casket, so that Sesame could drop it inside. "You were brill!"

Now the girls knew what the magic crystals looked like, it didn't take long to spot the other two. Maddy found the second one, and Sesame the third. But as she placed it in the casket . . .

CRACK! CRACK! CRACK!

The frozen lake splintered beneath their feet.

Can you crack the code and arrange the symbols to make a word? Each symbol represents a letter. If you solve the puzzle correctly, you'll help the Charmseekers find the snowflake charm!

Clue:
It looks like a pillar of ice!

A – heart	**N** – mermaid
B – horseshoe	**O** – butterfly
C – star	**P** – gate
D – crown	**Q** – sun
E – dolphin	**R** – moon
F – pumpkin	**S** – troll
G – fairy	**T** – cat
H – key	**U** – witch
I – candle	**V** – tree
J – coin	**W** – snowflake
K – unicorn	**X** – dragon
L – shell	**Y** – lantern
M – clover	**Z** – flower (poppy)

Seven

The girls sprang from one slab of ice to another. As they jumped on each one, symbols appeared in the ice.

"I think it's a code," said Maddy, springing to the next slab.

"Yes," said Sesame, landing beside her. "It looks like the one on my jewellery box!"

"I counted ten," said Maddy, as she sprang from the last slab onto firm ground.

"But they're melting! Quick, Ses. Tell me what they are. I'll draw them."

Maddy hunted around and found a sharp stone, then she drew the symbols as Sesame called them out.

Together they cracked the code.

"STALAGMITE," said Sesame. "I'm sure it's a clue to finding the charm."

"R-i-g-h-t," said Maddy. "Um, what exactly *is* a stalag-thingamy?"

"You find them in caves," said Sesame vaguely. "But I can never remember if they go up or down!"

They retraced their steps along the rocky passageways, looking high and low for the charm. Sesame was convinced they would find the snowflake charm but, to her dismay, they reached the mouth of the cave without finding anything. Disappointed, the girls stopped to catch their breath and Sesame checked her watch. The two moons were moving ever closer together!

"We're running out of time," she told Maddy. "If we don't find the charm soon, we'll have to—"

She broke off, as icy goose pimples prickled her spine and her necklace tingled as before.

"Oh, Maddy," she said, clapping her hand to her forehead. "I've been so stupid! That voice in my head saying 'pillars of ice'! It wasn't a warning. It was a *clue*. And a stalagmite is just like a—"

"—Pillar of ice!" said Maddy, who had twigged the link between the clues straightaway.

They turned and looked again at the strange ice formations. Only then did Sesame see what she had missed the first time – the precious little silver snowflake charm, frozen inside the biggest stalagmite of all.

She felt a mixture of elation and frustration.

"How are we going to get it out?" she said. "The ice is so thick."

Maddy gave the pillar a kick.

"Ouch!"

"Ssh!" said Sesame. "What was that?"

"My foot—" began Maddy. And stopped.

Together they felt the floor vibrate, then the bulk of something unimaginably big entered the cave. Sesame stifled a scream and grabbed hold of Maddy. A gigantic bear was standing on its hind legs, towering over them.

Hot breath steamed from its muzzle and gaping jaws revealed rows of sharp, white teeth. The Charmseekers had come face to face with Karvig the Snow Bear!

"What are you doing in MY cave!" growled Karvig.

"P-p-please," said Sesame. "We came to find the snowflake charm."

"And help the Ice Maiden," added Maddy, in a small, frightened voice.

At the mention of the gatekeeper's name, the Snow Bear's attitude changed dramatically.

"A-a-a-a-h, the Ice Maiden!" he said sadly, his warm breath filling the cave. "She is a good friend. But she is in a bad way. Soon she will be no more . . ."

"You must be Karvig!" said Sesame, remembering the gatekeeper had mentioned him. The girls introduced themselves and Maddy held up the glass casket for the bear to see.

"These crystals will stop the Ice Maiden melting," she said. "We must hurry or—"

"I shall take you to her at once!" said Karvig.

But Sesame held up her hand.

"I'm not leaving without the charm!" she said firmly, and showed Karvig where it was trapped. The Snow Bear looked at the glittering snowflake encased in its prison of ice and shook his head in disbelief.

"A charm in my cave? Right under my nose!" he said. "I think I can help you set it free."

He took deep breaths and breathed out hot, steamy air again and again. Gradually the pillar of ice began to melt and it went on melting, until Sesame could reach the precious charm and release it.

"At last!" she said, holding the perfect little silver snowflake in the palm of her hand. For a few minutes they all admired its filigree pattern and saw how it shimmered with a magical light of its own, then Sesame put it safely in her pocket.

"*Now* we can go!" she said.

Eight

Zorgan had not been prepared for the Silversmith's ability to read his mind.

"Hm!" he murmured. "I should not have underestimated her mystic powers. In a careless moment I allowed her to gain an insight into my thoughts. Blatz!* Now she knows some of my plans. I *must* get Sesame's locket somehow."

When the magician peered into his crystal ball, he couldn't believe his luck. There was Sesame and her friend. They were in the Ice Country, riding on a Snow Bear.

* * * * * * *
*Blatz – a really angry exclamation

"Ah-ha!" he cried. "My chance has come, sooner than I thought . . ."

"That was SO scary!" said Maddy, when they were safely over the crevasse. She looked back at the ice bridge shimmering in the moonlight, where on either side, depths of nothingness had been ready to swallow them up. Maddy had one arm wrapped around Sesame's waist; in the other she held the casket, containing the three crystals. Sesame half-turned and nodded.

"Yeah!' she said. "I'm glad that's over." Her cheeks were glowing from the cold night air. She looked up at the two moons, drifting across the sky. "Will we make it in time, Karvig?"

"I'll do my best," said the Snow Bear.

Karvig had insisted on taking the Charmseekers to the gate. He knew the way like the back of his paws, and as they went along he talked:

"I want to help the Ice Maiden. And the sooner all the magical charms are together again, the better. Our lives depend upon it! Until that day, my beloved Ice Country remains in danger of being destroyed. Grrr! If only I could get my teeth into the cursed magician who started all this—"

"Do you mean Zorgan?" Sesame asked.

She buried her hands in Karvig's long fur. It was warm and had a musky smell.

Karvig snorted in disgust.

"That's the one," he said. "Ha! I know a story about *him*!"

"Go on," said Maddy. "We'd love to hear it."

"It happened one moonlit night," he began. "It was autumn, in the mede of Arez. The first snow had fallen and the two moons were casting their silvery-blue light over everything. It was a perfect night for hunting! I set off through the forest, hoping to pick up the scent of my supper. After a while I saw my friend Talisk, the clawbeak,* hovering in the sky—"

"Excuse me," said Sesame. "What is a clawbeak?"

"A bird with snowy white wings," said Karvig. "Talisk's eyes are so sharp she can spot a whisker twitch. She doesn't miss a thing! I couldn't find anything in the forest that night, so I walked until I reached the edge of the Ice Country. And that's when I saw it."

* *

* **Clawbeak** – a type of eagle. This majestic bird lives in the Snowflake Mountains of the Ice Country

"What?" asked Maddy.

"The black tower," said Karvig. "It rose from the ground, like a cobra ready to strike. I saw Zorgan throwing what *looked* like stars from the top. I knew it was Zorgan, because my mother had told me stories about him when I was a cub. I remember there was one about the Sky Dancers. That's what we call the flashing lights in the sky. You may have seen them?"

"Yes," said Sesame. "They're amazing."

"Well," Karvig continued. "My mother said that whenever I saw them, I should think of Zorgan in his dark tower casting spells. She said he was trying to challenge the beauty of the Sky Dancers and gain more power for himself. So that night, when I saw him flinging stars about, I said to myself, 'Ah,

Zorgan is making magic. I must take care!' I only discovered my mistake later. Those weren't stars. They were charms!"

"Oh!" exclaimed Sesame. "So *that's* how they were lost. But why did he throw them away?"

Karvig grunted.

"Good question," he said. "Only Zorgan knows the answer to that!"

"How did you find out they *were* charms?" asked Maddy.

"I met Talisk on my way home," said Karvig. "By then we'd both had a good night's hunting and there was time to talk. She told me she'd counted thirteen silver charms, flying like shooting stars all over Karisma."

Maddy groaned.

"No wonder they're so hard to find!" she said.

Sesame felt the snowflake charm lying safely in her pocket.

"But we *will* find them," she said confidently.

The beasts took them all completely by surprise. They came out of nowhere, their eyes red as hot coals and their piercing screeches cutting the air, like a knife.

"Shriekers!" * growled Karvig. "I might have known. Hold tight!"

There were three of them, all females – the ruthless hunters of the pack. For a while they had been waiting, crouching low, watching the Snow Bear steadily lolloping across the snowfields towards them. Food was scarce and they were hungry! The bear was huge, but they judged they could take him on. And when the time was right – they SPRANG!

* *
* Shriekers – ferocious wild dogs like wolves, so called because of the high-pitched shriek they make in full cry

Sesame and Maddy screamed as the leader leaped at Karvig's throat. They clung on as the Snow Bear reared, slashing with his blue-black claws and sending the shrieker flying. The other two circled Karvig, trying to confuse him. Suddenly one of them darted in and snapped at his leg, so Sesame kicked out as hard as she could. She caught the shrieker *smack* on the nose and saw it fall back, yelping. Meanwhile Maddy was doing her best to scare the third one off by shouting.

"Go away! *Shooo! SHOOO!*

SHOOO!"

Karvig's fury at being attacked only added to his strength. He snarled and took on all three shriekers at once, swiping, biffing and punching them with his paws, like the prizefighter he was. It didn't take them long to realise they were no match for the bear, and with shrieks and yelps they ran off to their den to lick their wounds.

"Hooray!" cried Sesame and Maddy.

"I don't think they'll be bothering us again," said Karvig. "Now, let's get on. We're nearly there!"

Sesame glanced at her watch. She reckoned they had about five minutes before the Meeting of the Moons!

Nine

In her workshop at the foot of Mount Fortuna, the Silversmith lit a tinder-stick of mystica.✱ Soon the air filled with a fragrant aroma, which calmed her. Since her mind-battle with Zorgan, her thoughts have been racing. She has been gripped by a sense of foreboding, because she knows her Seeker is in great danger. Her fear of what might happen if Zorgan were to succeed trickles down her spine like melted ice.

"I *must* help her," said the Silversmith, placing her fingertips to her temples. She closed her eyes and concentrated her energies on Sesame and her

* *

✱**Mystica** — an aromatic plant, native to Karisma. The petals produce a sweet smell when burned

silver locket, then murmured, half in a trance: "If only I can reach her. Are my powers strong enough? I must put them to the test . . ."

Meanwhile Zorgan was observing the Charmseekers' progress through his powerful telescope. He had been biding his time, waiting for the right moment to strike. So when, by chance, the shriekers attacked the Snow Bear, the magician was delighted.

"Spallah!" * he exclaimed, stepping back from the spyglass to plot his next move. The pixie, Dina, stood alert, waiting for his command.

"Those mangy beasts will soon bring the bear down," muttered Zorgan, rubbing his hands with glee. "Then the Charmseekers will have to *walk* to the gate." He turned to fix Dina with a terrifying glare. "So, you'll have plenty of time to snatch Sesame's locket!"

"Yes, Master!" said Dina, her eyes glinting with eager anticipation. She couldn't wait to carry out her mission. "Leave Sesame Brown to me—"

* *
* Spallah – excellent! A triumphant expression

69

"Wait!" cried Zorgan. He put one eye to the telescope again and was just in time to see the shriekers beating a hasty retreat. "Blatz!" he cursed. "The Snow Bear is stronger than I thought. I must do something to stop Sesame reaching the gate. Dina, go NOW! Bring me the locket. Woe betide you if you fail!"

As soon as Dina had gone, Zorgan opened his *Book of Foul Weather Spells* and hastily thumbed through the pages. When he'd found a spell to suit his purpose, he took a deep breath and began to intone:

"Come icy blast and stinging snow . . ."

The Ice Maiden waited anxiously for the Charmseekers to return. She knew the terrible risk they had been willing to take to save her. As she waited, she wondered if they had found the crystals. And if they had, would they get back in

70

time? Her strength was failing fast. The constant *drip, drip, drip* of her melt-water tears had weakened her, and with every drop that ran down her cheeks, she became weaker still. So, when she saw the girls riding on Karvig's back and fast approaching the gate, her hopes were raised – hopes that suddenly vanished before her eyes . . .

Only a grickle  ago she'd heard Sesame call out to her, and had seen Maddy holding up the casket with the crystals inside! Such a short distance separated them she could almost *feel* the coldness of the crystals through the glass. But out of the blue – out of a clear, cloudless night sky – came a howling wind

* *
✱ Grickle – about the same time as a second in our world

71

that
whipped the
snow into a violent
storm. When she looked again,
Sesame, Maddy and the Snow
Bear had disappeared in a blur
of white.

Zorgan's blizzard struck with
such force, it stopped the Snow
Bear in his tracks. Karvig could
barely see his paw in front of
his nose.

"I've known bad weather
in my time," he growled.
"But nothing like this!"

"Ow! That hurt,"
shrieked Maddy,
as a blast of
hailstones struck her
full in the face.

"I can't see a
thing," cried Sesame,
above the whistling of
the wind.

Then, out of the whiteness came Dina, her steely wings buzzing like an angry bee. Dina's sharp eyes spotted Sesame's locket, and she zoomed in to snatch it. Before Sesame realised what was happening, she felt a sharp tug at her neck.

"What the—?" she began.

"OWWWOOOO!"

howled Dina, recoiling. "That was HOT!"

Sesame peered through the whirling snowflakes, trying to catch a glimpse of her attacker. Then she saw a pixie with flaming red hair, blowing hard on her fingers.

"Dina!" she exclaimed. Her first thought was to protect the snowflake charm and she held it tight in her pocket. She'd had the misfortune to meet Dina twice before, when the pixie had tried to take the horseshoe and cat charms from her, so she knew how determined Dina could be. But when the pixie dived again at her throat, Sesame realised she was more interested in her necklace. Zorgan's other pixie, Nix, had tried to grab it the last time she was in Karisma. How odd, she thought, now doing her best to defend herself. Dina made to grab the locket and again she jinxed back, squealing.

The pixie was baffled. Sesame's locket was shimmering with heat. It was scorching hot! But I *must* get it, she told herself. She could hear Zorgan's threat ringing in her ears. 'Woe betide you if you fail!' She flew at Sesame once more, screaming at the top of her voice:

"Give me your locket! My master Zorgan MUST have it."

But Sesame was ready for her this time. She held on to her locket with the

74

pictures of her parents inside, and would not let go. It felt smooth to her touch and tingled, as if her mum and dad were close by. She could almost *feel* them giving her courage.

"Well, tell Zorgan he can't have it!" she cried.

And she gave Dina a push.

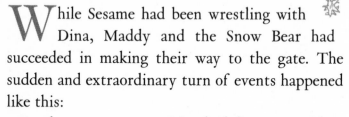

Ten

While Sesame had been wrestling with Dina, Maddy and the Snow Bear had succeeded in making their way to the gate. The sudden and extraordinary turn of events happened like this:

At the very moment Dina had first swooped to snatch Sesame's locket, Maddy noticed a change in the crystals. They had started to glow, and they grew brighter and brighter, until they dazzled her with their ice-blue brilliance.

"Fantastic!" she said. "They'll show us the way to the gate."

She slid off Karvig's back, clutching the casket. "Come on," she said to the Snow Bear. "We must hurry!"

The crystals shone a path of light through the raging blizzard and when they reached the gate, everything happened at once. Sesame pushed Dina away and jumped to the ground. She just had time to give Karvig a hug and whisper something in his ear, before running with Maddy to the gate.

"Thank you!" said the Ice Maiden, as Maddy handed her the casket. As soon as she opened the lid, the crystals burst into a shower of tiny freezing stars and swathed her in an icy mist. It was SO cold, it took the girls' breath away, but it stopped the beautiful maiden from melting. She beamed at the Charmseekers, as she held the gate open for them. "Did you find the snowflake charm?" she asked.

Sesame patted her pocket.

"Yes!" she said, her eyes sparkling with delight.

"I thought you would," said the Ice Maiden, with a knowing smile. "Now, hurry. It's time to go. Setfair,* Charmseekers. Come back soon!"

* *
* Setfair – goodbye and good luck

77

As Sesame and Maddy fell into a fluffy cloud of soft white snow they saw the two moons of Karisma slip one behind the other. The very last thing they heard was a roar from the Snow Bear, as Karvig sent Dina spinning, in a blast of hot air!

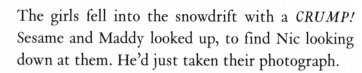

The girls fell into the snowdrift with a *CRUMP!* Sesame and Maddy looked up, to find Nic looking down at them. He'd just taken their photograph.

"Great!" he said. "This one's definitely for the front page."

Sesame struggled to her feet in a daze.

"No way, Dad!" she said. "I'd be SO embarrassed!"

"Me too," said Maddy, her head in a spin.

"Thought I'd lost you for a minute," he said, turning the camera round, to show them the picture. "Deep snowdrift! Anyway, time to go. I think you've had enough snow for one day."

Sesame and Maddy looked at each other. If only he knew what an amazing adventure they'd just had.

Later, after they'd taken Maddy home and Sesame was alone in her room, she took the precious silver snowflake from her pocket and looked at its delicate pattern again. Flashbacks of what they'd been through raced inside her head.

"But it was worth it!" she told Alfie, as she opened her jewellery box. Carefully she placed the glistening snowflake with the other six charms and the silver bracelet she'd already found and firmly closed the lid. "I know much more about these charms now," she said. "I can't wait to go back and look for the others! It's really important for the thirteen charms to be together, you see?

Terrible things are happening in Karisma because they've been lost. All because of that horrid magician Zorgan. I can't *believe* he threw them away!"

As soon as she said his name, images of her struggle with Dina flashed before her eyes. This was the second time one of Zorgan's pixies had tried to snatch her necklace, and she couldn't think why the magician would want it. It was weird the way it had burned the pixie too. She undid the clasp and laid her necklace beside her jewellery box. As she did so, the locket suddenly sprang open and there were the tiny pictures of her parents, smiling back at her.

Sesame looked at them fondly. She loved her dad *so* much, but she missed not having her mum around. She thought Poppy looked beautiful. Gently she closed the locket. It was one of her most treasured possessions.

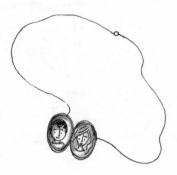

Eleven

The Silversmith goes to her window in time to see the two moons, passing one behind the other.

"Quisto!"* she exclaims. "The Meeting of the Moons. Who knows what strange things have happened beneath your beams this night?"

She turns from the window, and as she looks at the thirteen magic candles, she gives a sigh of relief.

"One thing I know for sure," she says. "The snowflake charm has been found!" For she sees the flame of the candle that bears its name has died. Now six candles remain burning brightly, six glowing beacons of hope that will burn until their charms have been found.

The Silversmith reflects on her exhausting encounters with Zorgan earlier in the day.

* * * * * * * * * * * * * * * * *

*Quisto – an exclamation of surprise

82

"I thwarted his attempts to discover where Sesame is keeping the charms," she says to herself. "Perish the day he ever finds out about the jewellery box! He will stop at nothing to possess the charms. Worse still, if he *should* get hold of Sesame's locket—"

A shiver runs down her spine. The consequences are too awful to think about. But she draws comfort from knowing she's protected her Seeker – this time. She allows herself a smile of satisfaction, as she imagines how surprised Dina must have been to burn her fingers on the locket.

Perhaps Zorgan's little pixie won't be quite so eager next time, she thinks. Although she fears deep down there *will* be a next time, and that Sesame remains in great danger, as she continues her quest.

But that is another story! It must be told another day.

Secret
Treasure

For Rosemary Sandberg, with love — A.T.

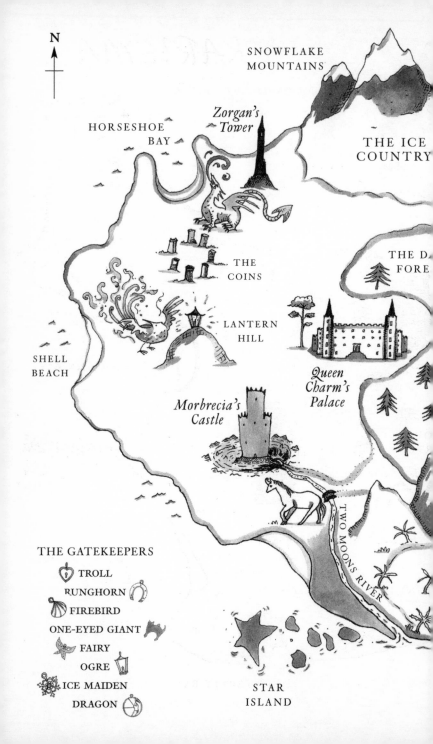

KARISMA

CAPE CAT

CLOVER FIELDS

HEARTMOOR

DOLPHIN BAY

OUNT
RTUNA

The Silver Pool

KEY
POINT

SWAMPS

JUNGLE

MERMAID
ROCK

BUTTERFLY BAY

One

"Who is Jason Flook?" asked Lois Brown, over supper one evening. Lois was Sesame's gran, but everyone called her Lossy. She tried to conceal a smile, as she spoke to her granddaughter.

"G-r-a-n," Sesame groaned. "Jason Flook is only *the* most gorgeous film star ever! You must have heard of him. He was the coolest pirate captain in *Treasure Seekers* and now he's making this brill new film—"

Sesame stopped when she saw Lossy exchange amused glances with her dad, Nic. "Oh, very funny, Gran. I might have known you were teasing!"

"Sorry," said Lossy. "Yes, of course I know who Jason Flook is. Just think! You might meet him tomorrow."

"Ooo, Dad!" said Sesame, hardly able to breathe she was so excited. "Do you think I will?"

"I'll try and fix it," said Nic. "On one condition. Promise me you won't faint. I don't want you to ruin a good picture!"

They had been talking about Star Productions' new action-packed adventure, *Tomb Robbers*. It was being filmed on location near an ancient burial site, and Nic had been booked for a photo shoot. The job fell during half-term, so he'd arranged for Sesame and her friends to come too.

After supper, Sesame raced upstairs to her room and chatted to Maddy, Gemma and Liz online:

seekerSes@zoom.com says:
Hi, everyone! Ready to meet You Know Who? Wot R U wearing? I can't decide!

MadWebbgirl@mailwizard.net says:
Yeah. We must look super glam for J.F. Ha, ha! Eeek! I've dropped a fake nail on the carpet.

funkygemG@helloo.com says:
Your dad's super-cool, Ses. Can't beleeeve I'm going on a film set. Celebs here we come! I'm soooo excited.

charmLizzy@chat2U.com says:
Me too. Won't sleep a wink tonight.
What time are we meeting at your house, Ses?
seekerSes@zoom.com says:
Come at 9. Dad says be on time (MadWebbgirl!)
See you all 2moz. Mwah Mwah x

Next morning, everyone arrived at Sesame's house on time – even Maddy! The girls piled into Nic's car, chatting excitedly. It took over an hour to drive to the location – a wild sweeping moor, famous for its ancient standing stones. On the way, the girls talked non-stop about their favourite pop stars, music, TV and film celebs, clothes, make-up and hair.

"Phew!" said Nic, when they eventually arrived. "It's amazing what you girls find to talk about!"

An attractive young woman holding a clipboard waved to them across the car park and came over. She had long black hair and was wearing a bright yellow top, skinny jeans and funky trainers.

"Hi!" she greeted them. "I'm Samira. Director's Assistant."

93

After introductions
Samira said:

"I'll show the girls around,
Nic. We'll meet up after the photo
shoot. Okay?"

"Great," said Nic. "Have fun."

Sesame, Maddy, Gemma and Liz followed
Samira through a jumble of trucks, trailers,
catering vans, cameras, cables and lighting
equipment. There were film crew
and technicians everywhere;
a man from the wardrobe
department carrying an armful
of costumes; a hair stylist spraying
a wig; noisy carpenters building scenery

and actors studying their scripts and rehearsing their lines. There was so much to take in all at once! Sesame couldn't resist asking the one question they'd all been longing to know the answer to:

"Where's Jason Flook?"

Before Samira had time to reply, some riggers came along manoeuvring a golden dragon. The huge prop was on a trolley and men were hauling it with ropes.

"Mind your backs!" shouted one.

Samira jumped out of the way, but Sesame stepped backwards and tripped over a trailing rope . . .

"Whoooops!" she cried.

"Steady there," said a gentle voice.

Sesame looked up to see a gorgeous young man with fair hair, deep blue eyes and a boyish face smiling down at her. It was Jason Flook!

"Here," said Jason, offering Sesame his hand. "Let me help you."

"Er, th-thanks," said Sesame, blushing red as a radish.

Maddy, Gemma and Liz stood awestruck, jaws dropping, eyes open wide. Samira grinned at Sesame.

"You were saying?" she said.

The next few minutes whizzed by. Jason chatted and joked with the girls and signed their autograph books, until his mobile rang.

"Sorry. Got to dash," said Jason. "Photo shoot."

"Trust Dad!" murmured Sesame.

"Samira, could you show me the way?" said Jason.

"Of course," she said. "Back in five, girls!"

She left Sesame, Maddy, Gemma and Liz to look around the burial chamber set. There was a sarcophagus, ornately carved and flanked by fierce-looking monsters. All around it were scattered gold coins and behind it stood the dragon.

"I know this coffin thing is fake," said Maddy, daring to touch the sarcophagus. "But it looks so real."

Liz gave a little shiver.

"Mm," she said. "Spooky!"

"It's fascinating—" began Gemma, but catching sight of Sesame, she stopped. Sesame was swaying slightly and looked as if she might faint. "Are you okay?"

"My head's spinning," said Sesame. "Everything's going round and round." She felt a gentle breeze on her cheeks, then suddenly she was tumbling head-over-heels and falling into a magical mist. "Maddy! Gemma! Liz!" she heard herself cry, only her voice seemed a million miles away. Next thing she knew, the others were flying with her through a cascade of silvery stars. They were on their way to Karisma!

Two

W hen Dina returned from the Ice Country, Zorgan had ranted and raged at her. He'd sent the pixie on a mission to snatch Sesame's locket, and she'd failed – just like Nix. As a punishment he ordered Dina to sit on the roof of his tower and repeat a million times: "I must not fail."

I must not fail I must not fail I must not fail

That was a mede✶ ago, and she was *still* chanting!

Now the magician paced the floor of his Star Room, vengeful thoughts swirling inside his head.

"I must have Sesame's locket!" he told Vanda, his pet bandrall.✶✶ The bird-like creature had perched on his shoulder and Zorgan was stroking her scraggy neck. "If I had hold of Sesame's locket, I could put her under a spell. Then she'd be compelled to bring ME all the charms. Hm! I must think of a way to get it . . ."

* *
✶ Mede – month
✶✶ Bandrall – rare flying mammal, native to Karisma

Zorgan considered how best to achieve this aim without anyone suspecting him. He had once tried (unsuccessfully) to turn his old enemy, the Silversmith, against Sesame Brown.

"Pah!" he snorted, remembering the Silversmith's angry response. "I might have known she'd defend her Seeker to the end. But maybe I could persuade Queen Charm instead? If *she* suspected Sesame of stealing her charms, she'd order Sesame's arrest. And if Sesame were held prisoner in the palace, I'd have a chance to snatch her locket. Well, not me. I'd transform Morbrecia into a spider again, so she could steal it! It worked with Charm's bracelet. I'm sure Morbrecia would fall in with my plans. But first I must deal with Charm . . . "

Zorgan hurried down a spiral staircase, one hundred and ninety five twisty steps, to his library. His vast collection of books on magic had once been ruined by drakons* – a spiteful act of revenge by Agapogo, he recalled, and all because he'd invoked the dragon to drain the Silver Pool. It had taken him time (and a considerable number of spells!) to restore his beautiful room full of books.

* *
*Drakon – a large, fire-breathing insect

Zorgan looked at the thousands of
volumes on the shelves and it gave
him great pleasure. Every
one of the leather-bound
books had been
dusted by Nix,

which had
been *her*
punishment
for failing to
steal Sesame's
locket! He scanned
the shelves, until one
particular title caught his attention:

RARE CHANTS AND INCANTATIONS
* REVISED EDITION *
New and improved spells for every occasion

he read on the cover. He opened it, flicked through the
pages till he came to page one hundred and fifty nine.

SEEDS OF DOUBT
A powerful spell, which sows seeds of doubt or suspicious thoughts in the mind of another. The unsuspecting recipient of these

159

intoxicating flowers will experience a complete change of mind about someone or something, within a few grickles * of smelling their scent.

160

"Perfect!" he said. "I'll try it at once!"

After adding names and a few details to the spell, Zorgan intoned these words over a handful of seeds:

> Seeds of doubt, grow into flowers,
> A sweet bouquet of magic powers.
> Fragrant scent, swell every bloom,
> Fill Charm's head with thoughts of gloom!
> Let doubts, like shadows, cross her mind;
> Her trust in Sesame has been blind.
> Let it be Charm's belief;
> The girl is nothing but a thief!

* *
Grickle — about the same time as a second in our world

102

The last word had barely left the magician's lips, when the seeds burst into a magnificent bouquet of dark purple flowers.

"Spallah!"* exclaimed Zorgan, clapping his hands. "Now for a suitable time to send them to Charm. I don't want to arouse her suspicions."

Glancing at his calendar he realised that this was the mede of Elar, when the queen celebrated her birthday. As luck would have it, today was the day! Quickly Zorgan conjured a birthday card, wrote a greeting then sent it and the flowers to the palace.

* *

* Spallah — excellent! A triumphant expression

Three

Sesame landed with a bump beside a wall, which had a row of shiny spikes along the top. At least that's what she thought they were, until they twitched. Seconds later, Maddy, Gemma and Liz landed nearby.

Thump, thump, thump!

"What the—?" began Maddy, picking herself up and peering at the pinkish-silvery scales, glinting in the early morning sun.

"It's a t-t-tail," said Sesame. "I saw it move."

"Gross!" said Gemma.

Liz gulped and pointed. "Look!"

The girls looked where she was pointing, along the length of the tail, which was attached to an enormous body. Two leathery wings were folded across the back and at the end of a very long neck, there was the head of – a dragon! The dragon was snoring loudly and, with each snuffling snort, he blew a blast of hot air in their direction. To everyone's horror, he suddenly opened one eye and seemed very surprised to see them.

"Hurrumph! Ahem! Um, well now," he began, in a I-wasn't-really-asleep sort of way. "Where did *you* come from?"

Sesame hid a smile. It was obvious the dragon was embarrassed to have been caught snoozing. She introduced everyone and told him they were from a world a long way away.

"Ahhhhh!"

said the dragon, hissing steam from his nostrils like a pressure cooker. "You're Charmseekers! Fairday.*
Welcome to Karisma! I'm Pogo, Gatekeeper Eight. You're the first visitors to come through my gate. I've never met anyone from the Outworld**
before."

They were standing outside Pogo's cave and Gemma noticed a roll of parchment on the ground.

* *
*Fairday – a typical Karisman friendly greeting
**Outworld – the name Karismans call our world

"What's that?" she asked.

Pogo seemed delighted to show it to her.

"My family tree!" he said. "It's a bit scorched, I'm afraid. Do you know, I can trace my family back to Agapogo."

"Cool!" said Sesame. She remembered the time she and Maddy had been told the Legend of the Silver Pool.✶ "Agapogo was the poor dragon who drowned in silver, wasn't she?"

✶ ✶
✶ The Legend of the Silver Pool – do you remember the story? You'll find it in *Book Two: The Silver Pool*

"Yes," said Pogo. "I'm very proud of my ancestor. I wish I knew more about her. There was a time when we dragons—"

Sesame was afraid he would keep them talking about dragons all day, so she quickly changed the subject.

"We've come to look for the charms that are still lost," she said.

"Oh, the magical charms!" said Pogo wistfully. "Which ones?"

"The key, dolphin, star, moon, cloverleaf and coin," replied Sesame.

"Hm, the silver coin . . ." said Pogo dreamily. He yawned. "There's a ring of standing stones called The Coins. You might start looking there?" He yawned again and his eyelids drooped.

Sesame had a feeling they *might* find the coin there. Anyway it was worth a try.

"How will we find them?" she asked.

"Map," said Pogo sleepily. He produced a crumpled map from under his wing and gave it to Sesame. "Be sure to be back by the Seventh Shadow—"

The last word trailed away.

"What does *that* mean?" asked Maddy.

But Pogo had fallen asleep. The Charmseekers would have to work it out for themselves!

Sesame spread out the map, so they could all see where they were. Maddy spotted a circle of dots.

"I reckon they must be the standing stones," she said.

"Oh, look," said Liz, pointing to four specks of light.

"That's us!" said Sesame. "They track our position. I had a map like this, the first time I came to Karisma."

"Wicked!" said Gemma.

And they set off to look for The Coins.

On the way, they noticed a tall, dark tower in the distance.

"Ooo!" said Maddy. "I think that's Zorgan's tower. Ses, remember what the Snow Bear told us, when he helped us in the Ice Country?"

"Yes," said Sesame. "If you're right, it's where Zorgan threw the charms away!"

"What *are* you talking about?" asked Gemma.

"Come on, tell us," said Liz.

So Sesame and Maddy told them what they'd found out about Zorgan, the last time they came to Karisma. By the time they'd finished, they had come to a grassy mound swathed in morning mist. They could just make out the blurred outline of a standing stone, rising eerily from the ground, and when they went to investigate they found the lower part of the stone had some carvings, partly covered by moss. Liz scraped the moss away and discovered a number with some strange words carved below it.

At first none of them could make any sense of it, but Sesame loved puzzles and cracking codes and soon saw a way to solve this one.

Standing Stone Message:
Can you see what Sesame read in the mirror?

"Has anyone got a mirror?" she said. "I think this is mirror-writing!"

"Here," Maddy said. "Have mine."

Sesame wrote the words in her autograph book, near Jason Flook's signature. Seeing his name suddenly took her back to the set of *Tomb Robbers*. It all seemed so far away now, but the film location had been near an ancient burial mound. Weird! Meanwhile, Gemma couldn't contain her excitement.

"Wow! Treasure!" she cried. "I bet there's an entrance somewhere—"

She stopped. Sesame was frowning and pointing to the words on the standing stone.

"Gemma, don't be crazy. It says *cursed* treasure! It's a warning. Anyway, we must find another charm. The coin might be here."

"Oh, don't be such a spoilsport," said Gemma. "We're standing on buried treasure! Come on. We can look for the charm later."

"No way!" said Sesame. "You don't understand. Horrible things are happening in Karisma because Zorgan threw the charms away. And they'll get worse until the charms are found. We haven't got time to look for stupid treasure and mess about with dragon bones!"

Maddy nodded. "I agree," she said. "I'm with you, Ses."

"Oh, surprise, surprise," said Gemma, goggling her eyes. "How about you, Liz? Are you coming?"

Liz's glasses had steamed up and she took them off to give them a wipe. She hated arguments! While Sesame and Gemma had been squabbling, she'd been thinking about the inscription on the stone. It *was* intriguing . . .

"Well?" demanded Gemma.

"Okay," said Liz. "I'll come."

Four

Charm was up bright and early on the morning of her birthday. After breakfast, she went to the window and looked out. Despite all the trouble in Karisma, the sun was shining and she was looking forward to seeing her friends later, to celebrate. There was a tap on the door and her maid Ozina came in.

"Good morning, Your Majesty," she said. "Happy Birthday! You've got lots of cards this morning. And these flowers have just arrived."

She presented Charm with a bouquet of dark purple blooms.

"Oh, how beautiful!" said Charm. "I wonder who sent them?" She saw the card and read:

To Her Majesty,
Happy Birthday!
from a well-wisher
x x

"Curious," said Charm. "I don't recognise the handwriting." Then somehow she couldn't resist burying her nose in the petals. "Mm! They have a lovely smell."

And she inhaled their intoxicating scent.

As Ozina left the room, she bumped into Dork, who was on guard duty in the corridor.

"I think Her Maj has got a secret admirer!" she told him.

It took no time at all for the spell to work. As Charm opened her birthday cards, her head began to ache and she found herself thinking about Sesame. And the more her head ached, the more she thought about Sesame, until she thought she had a headache because Sesame was stealing her charms! Dreadful thoughts about the Silversmith's special Charmseeker buzzed like wasps in her head.

Charm twisted a strand of hair round her finger. She was having serious doubts about the judgement of her dearest friend. Could the Silversmith, who she trusted completely, have been wrong about Sesame? Charm had believed her when she'd said Sesame had a gift to seek and find her charms. Perhaps Sesame had a gift for keeping them too! Where *was* her silver bracelet? Where *were* the charms Sesame had found? In the Outworld, that's where! How could the Silversmith be so sure her Seeker would bring them back?

Charm crossed the room and flung the door open.

"Organise a search party," she ordered Dork. "Next time Sesame Brown comes to Karisma, arrest her. My sister was right. The girl is a thief!"

Dork saluted smartly.

"Yes, Your Majesty," he said. "Happy Birthday!"

Dork was pleased to be back in the queen's good books, although he couldn't think how it had come about. When he'd tried to arrest Sesame near Butterfly Bay, Charm said he'd made a terrible mistake. Well, he thought, orders are orders. It's not for me to question Her Maj. My duty is to obey and *this* time I won't let Sesame get away.

Later that morning Dork and his soldiers were passing Morbrecia's castle. He spotted Morbrecia high on the battlements, peering through a small telescope.

The princess saw him too.

"What are you doing here?" she yelled. "I suppo my sister sent you to spy on me again? Well, tell I she won't be getting a birthday present from me!"

"N-n-no, Your Highness," stuttered Dork, craning his neck to speak to her. He was always a little afraid of the hot-tempered princess. "I have orders to arrest Sesame Brown."

"Really?" said Morbrecia. This was surprising news. "What's changed her mind?"

"Couldn't say," said Dork. "But Her Majesty says you were right to suspect Sesame. We're keeping a sharp look out for her return. Er, the view from your battlements must be excellent, Your Royal Highness. W-w-would you be k-k-kind enough to have a quick look for her?"

"Very well," snapped Morbrecia. It was precisely what she'd been doing anyway, but she didn't tell Dork. If Sesame *was* on the trail of another charm and happened to find one, she wanted to be there to grab it. She put the spyglass to her eye and saw a strange, dark cloud hovering over Charm's palace.

How odd, she thought. A purple cloud in a clear blue sky! But she thought no more of it because, just then, four moving figures caught her attention. They were walking near an ancient circle of standing stones . . .

"Vixee!"* she cried, punching the air. "The Charmseekers are back!"

* *
* **Vixee** – a gleeful, triumphant expression meaning 'great' or 'wicked'

118

Five

"I wonder why they're called The Coins?" said Maddy. "They don't *look* like coins."

"Haven't a clue," said Sesame, kicking at a tuft of grass. She was upset about quarrelling with Gemma, but she knew she was right. We're Charmseekers, she said to herself. We're here to look for the charms!

The early morning mist had cleared, revealing more standing stones – each with a number carved on the side. Sesame and Maddy had searched around six stones and were now standing by the last one – stone number seven.

"This one's taller than the rest," observed Maddy.

She thought no more of it because suddenly they both heard a startled cry. A few minutes later, Liz came running towards them, waving her arms.

"Come quickly!" she yelled. "It's Gemma. She needs our help!"

Sesame and Maddy didn't hesitate, they ran like the wind after Liz. She led them to a patch of ground that had given way.

"Gemma's fallen down there," she panted. "I called and called but there was no answer. What if she's—"

Sesame was already on her hands and knees, tearing at weeds and roots; the others helped her, until they'd cleared an opening. Liz feared the worse as they peered into the gloomy darkness of a deep shaft, which had foot and handholds in one wall.

"I'll climb down," said Sesame.

"Be careful!" said Maddy. "I'm coming with you."

"Me too," said Liz, trying to be brave.

But when they reached the bottom, there was no sight or sound of Gemma. She had completely disappeared.

"What about the map, Ses?" suggested Maddy. "Gemma *might* show up on it."

"Brill!" said Sesame. "Why didn't I think of that?"

Hastily, she unfolded the map. Sure enough, there was a solitary speck of light, weaving its way along a twisty passage.

"Oh, no!" wailed Liz. "Gemma's gone right inside. I'm scared. I can't go in there."

She began to cry, so Maddy tried to comfort her.

"It's okay," she said. "You stay here. I'll go with Ses. Your light on the map will help us find our way back."

"Thanks," said Liz.

They gave each other their secret Charmseekers hand sign for luck, before they parted.

Sesame and Maddy started along a narrow tunnel, following Gemma's illuminated speck on the map. All around them was a greenish half-light and the dreadful smell of rotten eggs.

"Pooo!" exclaimed Maddy, grabbing a hanky from her pocket and holding it over her nose.

Sesame coughed and spluttered.

"Yeah. Worse than gribblers,"* she said. "And they were bad enough!"

*Gribbler — extremely unpleasant goblin-like creature with yellow teeth and bad breath

Meanwhile Gemma was making her way towards a chamber at the centre of the burial mound. She seemed oblivious to the foul aroma filling the air. All she could hear were eerie voices inside her head, urging her on:

I am Smoulder, I am Fume,
Come into our ancient tomb!
Fortune hunter, have no fear,
The gold you seek is waiting here.

Gemma had fallen under the curse of two dragon spirits! She was like a sleepwalker, unaware of her surroundings or the dangers that lay ahead. But when she entered the burial chamber . . . it was as if a switch had been snapped on. Nothing could have prepared her for the sight that met her eyes. A glittering, gleaming hoard of gold filled the room – golden rings, goblets, coins, dishes, jewelled crowns and priceless treasures were piled high, from floor to ceiling. Her jaw dropped and her eyes sparkled with delight.

"Wicked!" she said.

And she reached for a big, shiny bracelet . .

Her fingers had barely touched the bangle, when there s a blinding flash of green light. Two terrifying dragon spectres rose from the treasure, their scales glowing in the gloom, their stinking breath engulfing her. Gemma jumped back and screamed, and once again their ghostly voices filled her head:

I am Smoulder,
I am Fume,
Welcome to our
ancient tomb!
If gold you seek, the price is high;
Your life, for ours — prepare to

DIE!

Six

Far away on Mount Fortuna, the Silversmith was getting ready to go to the palace. She had received an invitation from Queen Charm, to attend her birthday celebrations that evening.

> Her Majesty, Queen Charm of Karisma, requests the pleasure of your company at a party to celebrate The Queen's Birthday at Moonrise on the Eighth day of Elar.
>
> ⋙ The Palace ⋘

"I wish I could give Charm her bracelet," the Silversmith told a little bird, which had perched on her windowsill. "That would be the *best* birthday present!"

She sighed as she looked at the thirteen magic candles. Six remained burning brightly, waiting for their charms to be found. "I must be patient. My special Seeker has seven magical charms in her safekeeping and I have no doubt she'll find the others too, in time."

The Silversmith wandered into her garden to pick some poppies for the queen.

"If I can't give Charm her bracelet, I shall take her these instead." She tied them with a pretty ribbon. "There – flowers fit for a queen!" But as she said it, a sharp pain gripped her temples, like a vice.

"Hushish!"* she exclaimed. "Something is wrong."

The Silversmith hurried inside, her heart pounding.

"*Memora compozay tribulato!*" she said. It was an old saying, passed on through generations of Silversmiths. "Remember to keep calm in difficulties!"

She closed her eyes and an image of a swirling purple cloud swam into view. It was hovering right over the palace! Was it a bad omen? Was Charm ill? Perhaps she was in danger!

* *
*Hushish – a word used to express dismay

Suddenly the vision of Sesame broke through the haze, and now the Silversmith sensed her *Seeker* was in danger. Sesame was in Karisma, in a dark place associated with long-dead dragons!

The image wavered. She pressed her fingertips to her temples, the better to concentrate.

"Ah!" she sighed. "Sesame is wearing her locket. Good. And I see a silvery aura round her. If she *is* threatened by dragon ghosts, the aura will shield her."

Seven

"Aaaaaah!"

Sesame and Maddy froze when they heard Gemma's chilling scream. It pierced the silence of the tomb and sent shivers down their spines.

"Oh, Ses," Maddy whispered, her voice quivering. "Gemma's in trouble. I wonder what's happened?"

Sesame's stomach churned, her legs felt like jelly and she thought she was going to be sick. But as she stood there with Maddy, she felt her necklace tingle; her locket was warm on her skin and, quite unexpectedly, a surge of courage flowed through her. Sesame couldn't explain it, but she just *knew* she could face whatever lay ahead. She grabbed Maddy's hand.

"Come on," she said. "There's only one way to find out!"

They ran along the passageways, guided by Gemma's speck of light on the map, until they arrived at the entrance to the burial chamber. There they stopped, horrified by what they saw.

129

Gemma was standing, unable to move, as if held by some invisible force. Towering over her were the gruesome, ghostly forms of two enormous dragons, their jaws drawn back in triumphant leers!

Sesame gasped. The dragon spectres were about to strike Gemma! She *had* to do something . . .

Sesame SPRANG – putting herself between Gemma and the monstrous reptiles. Although she was completely unaware of it, Sesame's aura had a devastating effect on the dragons. She watched in stunned amazement as the grisly creatures recoiled, writhing in agony, their hollow eyes glowing like burning coals. At the same time, their wretched curse over Gemma was broken.

"Sesame!" cried Gemma, suddenly able to speak again. "Don't let them get you!"

The spectres were furious and their deafening roars shook the pillars of the chamber. Sesame shielded her face from the full blast of their fiery breath, as they roared:

I am Smoulder, I am Fume,
You dare disturb our ancient tomb!
Be gone Outworlder, leave us be,
We curse the name of
SESAME!

There was an ear-splitting

BOOM

followed by brilliant flashes of light, crackling and fizzing like fireworks. The girls felt the floor shake.

"Look!" yelled Maddy. "The roof is falling in! Run for it. Now!"

131

And they did. The three girls leaped from the burial chamber, as huge blocks of stone came crashing down. When the dust eventually settled and they dared look back, they could see no sign of the dragons, or the treasure – not even a single coin. Everything was buried under a heap of rubble.

For a moment, the girls stood in the dusty passageway, holding each other.

"Phew!" said Sesame. "I can't believe we got away from those ghastly . . . dragon ghosts."

"Yeah. They were scary!" said Maddy.

"I'm sorry," said Gemma. "It's all my fault! But when I fell down the shaft, something weird happened. I heard voices—"

Sesame suddenly remembered Liz, who was waiting for them at the foot of the shaft.

"Tell us later," she said. "We must get back to Liz.
She'll be wondering where we are!"

"Her light on the map will help us," said Maddy. "Let's have a look."

But when Sesame went to fish the map out of her pocket, she discovered it wasn't there.

"Oh, no! I must have dropped it in the burial chamber. There's no way we'll find it now."

"Well, we'll just have to manage without it," said Gemma. "I got us into this mess, so I'll get us out. Follow me!"

Burial Chamber Maze

Can you help Gemma, Sesame and Maddy find their way back along the maze of passages, to where Liz is waiting for them?

Eight

After watching Sesame and Maddy disappear down the dark passageway, Liz settled herself to wait for them. Her only comfort was the sunlight, streaming down from above and bathing her in a pool of light.

"I'd much rather *read* about secret treasure than go looking for it," she said to herself. She regretted her decision to go with Gemma. "Anyway I bet there's nothing here—"

Her attention was caught by something lying at the foot of the shaft. It was a roll of parchment, tied with a silver ribbon.

"What's this?" she said, picking it up and untying the bow. Carefully she unrolled the scroll and read what was written there:

I, Silvesta, Silversmith of Karisma, on this eighth day in the mede of Arez, this being the fiftieth year of The Gloom, bear witness to the events I have described here.

In the years known as The Gloom, there lived two monstrous dragons called Smoulder and Fume, who were brothers. For fifty years they held the good people of Karisma to ransom. Whether folk were rich or poor, they were forced to give up their silver and gold. Anyone resisting the demands of these greedy brothers paid a terrible price – their homes and crops were destroyed by the monsters' fiery breath, and in this way Smoulder and Fume each acquired vast hoards of treasure.

But in the fiftieth year of this sad time, when treasures were scarce to find, Smoulder and Fume grew envious of one another's ill-gotten gains, and each thought the other had more than his fair share.

One day they quarrelled over a handful of flukes* – just seven small coins. The quarrel turned into a fight, and the fight became a fierce battle! For seven days and seven nights the dragons grappled, clawed, clashed, brawled and blasted each other with red-hot flames, which scorched the land for as far as the eye could see.

On the seventh day of this dreadful contest, when both were weak and near to death, the selfish, heartless dragons made a pact. With their dying breath they cursed anyone who might come after them and disturb their bones to steal their treasure.

> "If gold you seek, the price is high;
> Your life, for ours – prepare to DIE!"

* *

* **Fluke** – a small gold coin (Karisman old money) in use before the existence of the Silver Pool

138

And with these words, they died – and so too ended the fifty years of misery in Karisma known as The Gloom.

Now Smoulder and Fume had a sister called Agapogo, who had nothing to do with her brothers' wicked ways. She was a feisty dragon and cared nothing for her brothers' dying curse. Besides, she knew full well that one dragon may not curse another – there is honour, even among dragons! So Agapogo took it upon herself to return all the stolen treasures to the people of Karisma, and invited them to reclaim their possessions. A few dared risk the dragons' curse, but most Karismans thought it unlucky to possess anything Smoulder and Fume had touched.

So I, Silvesta the Silversmith, having charge over all precious metals, ordered the unclaimed treasure to be buried deep inside this burial mound in a secret chamber, and the remains of Smoulder and Fume be placed there too.

In recognition of Agapogo's gesture of goodwill, our king, Umbriel, gave her a fine collection of silver ornaments. He knew how much Agapogo loved silver! I, myself, fashioned a beautiful silver goblet, which became Agapogo's most treasured possession. As I write, she guards her very own hoard of silver in a cave on Mount Fortuna and, apart from some occasional roars, I'm happy to say she doesn't bother anyone.

As for those seven flukes the dragons fought over? I threw them into the air and where they fell, seven standing stones appeared, which I called The Coins. And on the first stone I carved these words, as a warning to anyone foolish enough to disturb the dragons and their cursed gold!

1

IN A CIRCLE, SEVEN STONES,
GUARDIANS OF OLD DRAGON BONES.
CURSED TREASURE LIES BELOW,
WHERE ONLY FOOLISH FOLK DARE GO!

Then I hid the scroll in this place for safekeeping and whosoever shall find it, may know that this is a true record.

Silvesta the Silversmith

Liz had just finished reading, when Gemma appeared, followed by Sesame and Maddy.

"Oh, Liz," said Gemma. "I've never been so frightened in all my life! It was terrible. There were these two dragons—"

"—Smoulder and Fume," said Liz, waving the scroll. "I found this. It's all about them. You were SO lucky to get out. I think they put you under a curse!"

They scrambled up the shaft and out into the warm sunshine. After the cold, dark, foul-smelling tomb, it was a relief to be in the fresh air. Liz listened in awe, while the others told her about their horrifying ordeal in the burial chamber. Then she showed them the ancient scroll.

"Fantastic, Liz!" said Sesame, after she'd read it. "It's a brill find. Agapogo's silver has been a mystery, up till now. This explains everything!"

Liz beamed. She was pleased to have done *something* useful, while the others were facing such danger.

"Pogo will want to see this," she said. "He'll love reading about his ancestor."

"Okay," said Sesame. "But he can't keep it. He *must* give it to Queen Charm. It's an important part of Karisman history."

"Good thinking," said Gemma. "And talking of Pogo, isn't time we were getting back? The dragon said we must return by the Seventh Shadow, whenever *that* is. We still haven't a clue what it means."

"And we still haven't found a charm!" said Sesame.

Nine

Sesame looked at the sun lowering in the sky, and guessed they didn't have much time left before the gate closed.

"We *can't* go until we've found a charm," she said. "Maddy and I were at the seventh stone when you came for us, Liz. Come on. Let's all look there."

They retraced their steps to The Coins. The standing stones cast long shadows in the late afternoon sun, and as Maddy stood at the foot of the seventh stone, something twigged.

"Look," she said. "Its shadow is pointing to the gate. *This* is the Seventh Shadow! We must return before it reaches Pogo."

"You're right," said Gemma.

"It's getting longer," said Liz. "We won't have much time to look for the charm."

"I'm *sure* we'll find the coin here somewhere," said Sesame. She looked very determined. "Sesame Brown will track it down! Please, keep looking."

So the girls crawled around on their hands and knees, parting clumps of grass and looking under stones, until Gemma suddenly gave a squeal of delight.

"Here!" she cried. "I've found it. I've *found* it!"

The sun had struck the base of the stone and there, caught in a crack and glinting in the sunlight, was the coin charm. Gemma stooped to pick it up and held it in the palm of her hand. The others crowded round to admire the tiny silver coin, which bore the head of Queen Charm. It glistened with a light of its own.

"Oh," said Sesame. "How lovely!"

"Well done, Gemma," said Maddy.

"Totally brill!" said Liz.

Gemma heaved a sigh of relief and hoped it would make up for her quarrel with Sesame.

"This is the *best* treasure!" she said, handing the coin to her for safekeeping. And Sesame gave her a hug.

✶ ✶ ✶
✶

Meanwhile, the Charmseekers were being watched! Hidden behind the standing stones were Dork and his men, and hiding from them was Morbrecia.

144

When Dork saw Gemma hand the charm to Sesame, it was his cue for action. He leaped out, shouting:

"Sesame Brown! Stop in the name of Queen Charm. Once more I find you in possession of Her Majesty's property. Hand it over. You're under arrest!"

The girls gawped at him.

"Oh, not you again," muttered Maddy, under her breath.

"What *is* his problem?" murmured Gemma.

"NO WAY!" said Sesame, clasping the charm firmly in her fist. "I can't believe you're doing this. We're Charmseekers! Can't you see we're trying to help?"

Liz tugged at her sleeve. Out of the corner of her eye she'd caught sight of several soldiers advancing towards them.

Then Sesame saw them too, and someone else – the familiar figure of Morbrecia was lurking in the shadows. Sesame reckoned it was some kind of trap and she knew they had to act *fast*!

145

"Come on," she hissed to the others. "RUN!"

So the Charmseekers ran flat out, ahead of the lengthening Seventh Shadow. Sesame's quick reaction took Morbrecia completely by surprise.

"Blatz!" * she cursed. "Sesame mustn't get away with another charm."

And she pelted after Dork and his men, now chasing the Charmseekers in full cry . . .

* * *
*

Pogo had been waiting for the Charmseekers to return. As the Seventh Shadow crept ever closer to his gate, he was afraid they wouldn't make it. So it was a relief when, at last, he saw them racing towards him. But why were Dork and his soldiers pursuing them? And what was Princess Morbrecia doing? The gatekeeper was confused. Absent-mindedly, he swished his long, spiky tail from side to side. *SWISH. SWISH.* Tail swishing had become a habit, whenever Pogo tried to work things out.

* *
* **Blatz** – a really angry exclamation

SWISH, SWISH, SWISH!

"What's going on?" he said. "Why is everyone chasing the Charmseekers?"

SWISH!

"Hurry!" he shouted, when Sesame and the others were in earshot.

"We're coming!" yelled Sesame.

After that everything happened at once. Pogo flicked his tail and swept Dork and his men off their feet. The soldiers went flying in all directions!

Morbrecia ducked and plunged at Sesame; she saw she was wearing her locket, so she made a grab for it. But Maddy saw what Morbrecia was up to and pulled her hair, just as Gemma stuck out her foot and tripped the princess up.

"Magworts!" *screamed the furious Morbrecia, now lying flat on her back. She looked up in time to see Dork and his men staggering to their feet. "Doofers!"** she yelled. "Get after them!"

By now, Liz had reached the gate and was thrusting the parchment at Pogo.

"Here," she panted. "Take this. Give it to Queen Charm!"

And with one last effort, all four Charmseekers fell through the gate and into a cloud of mist and stars . . .

* *

*Magwort – probably the worst name you could call anyone! General term for a fool

**Doofer – idiot of the first order. Brainless

148

Dork was furious with Pogo.

"It's all your fault!" he shouted. "If it hadn't been for your stupid tail, we'd have caught Sesame and her gang of robbers. You should have stopped them."

Pogo looked bemused.

"There must be some mistake," he said. "They're Charmseekers. We gatekeepers have been told by Her Majesty to give them every assistance."

"Well, *I'm* under orders from Her Majesty to arrest them!" said Dork. "They're thieves and you've just helped them to escape. Her Maj will not be pleased, I can tell you."

"Yes, she will," said Pogo brightly. "Give her this." He fished the scroll from under his wing. "Historic document. It contains some very important information about Agapogo. *My* ancestor! I guarantee Queen Charm will be *very* pleased when she reads it."

"Hm," said Dork. "Well, I suppose it's better than nothing."

And he marched off to the palace.

Morbrecia meanwhile had taken the opportunity to slip away to her castle; every step of the way she cursed Sesame for thwarting her yet again.

"I'll be ready next time," she vowed. "Then Sesame Brown had better watch out!"

149

Ten

The girls landed back on the set of *Tomb Robbers*. Seconds later, Samira returned from taking Jason Flook to the photo shoot.

"Hope you weren't bored while I was away," she said.

The four girls exchanged knowing glances. If only Samira knew! Sesame thought their adventure would make a fantastic film but, of course, they couldn't tell anyone about it – yet. She smiled at Samira, as she reached into her pocket to finger the precious little coin charm, and said:

"No. We've had a great time."

"Yeah, loads to see," said Maddy truthfully.

"And do," added Gemma.

"Mm, loads," agreed Liz, wiping silvery mist from her glasses.

"Fab!" said Samira. She turned to Sesame. "Your dad wants to take a picture of you all with Jason and the cast. Follow me, girls!"

So they trooped after Samira to a real standing stone, where Jason and his co-stars were posing for pictures. At the end of the session, Nic lined everyone up for a final shot. I must be dreaming, thought Sesame, as she stood next to Jason.

"SMILE!" said Nic.

And Sesame smiled all the way home.

Later that evening, when Sesame was getting ready for bed, she thought about some of the extraordinary things that happened that day. She looked at the photograph her dad had taken, earlier.

"Look," she told her teddy, Alfie. "There's me with top celeb, Jason Flook!"

But feelings of happiness were mingled with sadness, when her thoughts turned to Karisma. The special jewellery box lay open on her beside table; Sesame was proud to have found eight of the thirteen lost charms and to have put them here for safekeeping, with Queen Charm's bracelet. She couldn't resist taking them out now and admiring them, one by one: the heart with its tiny keyhole; the horseshoe, shell and cat; the delicate little butterfly she'd found in a spider web; the lantern and the snowflake. And now the charming silver coin with its image of the queen . . .

As Sesame replaced the charms in the box and closed the lid, thoughts about Queen Charm whirled inside her head. She felt puzzled and upset.

"Why has the queen turned against me?" she said. "Charm sent Dork to arrest me. She thinks I'm *stealing* her charms! But she must know that's SO not true. It's not fair! I'm doing my best to help her. And I've still five more charms to find—"

Alfie slid sideways off the pillow, so Sesame propped him up again. She unclasped her necklace, and suddenly a vision of Morbrecia flashed in front of her. Sesame remembered how she'd seen the princess lurking near The Coins, and how she'd tried to snatch her locket.

"I wish I could tell Charm about her sister!" she told Alfie. "*She's* the one who ought to be under arrest. Morbrecia is after the charms and she tried to take my locket.  Zorgan wants them too. I bet they're working together. Oh, Alfie, it's all *so* confusing!"

For the next few moments, Sesame held her necklace in the palm of her hand. It was very special to her, but why were Zorgan and Morbrecia so keen to have it? The necklace felt warm and tingly to her touch. How weird, she thought. It's as though someone has been listening to what I've been saying! She opened the locket and there were the pictures of her mum, Poppy, and her dad, smiling back at her. Seeing them made her feel much better.

Carefully, she placed the necklace beside her bed and switched off the light. Somehow, she thought, as she snuggled under her duvet, things would work out okay. One day. Until then, she couldn't wait to go back to Karisma to find the missing charms!

153

Eleven

It was nearly Moonrise and the queen's birthday celebrations were about to begin. Charm had arranged a modest party – not too grand – to which she had invited one hundred important officials and special friends. Ozina was helping Charm with her dress – a shimmering turquoise and emerald gown, covered with sequins.

"Karisma is going through difficult times," said Charm, placing a filigree silver coronet on her head. "Until my charm bracelet has been found, things are unlikely to get better. Which reminds me, I still have the dreadful headache I had this morning!"

"Oh dear, Your Majesty," said Ozina, and tried to think of something to cheer her up. It didn't take long. "Cook's made you a lovely birthday cake!"

Charm smiled.

"Well," she said, "I shall save a piece for you."

The Silversmith was among the first guests to arrive. She stepped out of her horse-drawn carriage in front of the palace gates and gave a little gasp of surprise.

The strange purple cloud that had appeared in her vision, was hanging over the palace. I wonder what it means? she thought, as she hurried inside.

Crossing the elegant ballroom, hung with sparkling chandeliers, she greeted Charm with a curtsey.

"Happy Birthday, Your Majesty," she said. But the Silversmith was dismayed to see her friend looking agitated and concerned, and knew at once something was wrong.

"I must talk to you about Sesame Brown," said Charm, keeping her voice low, and took the Silversmith aside. "I'm convinced your Seeker is a thief! I've ordered Dork to arrest her. There's no mistake this time."

The Silversmith was horrified.

"Oh, but you *are* mistaken," she ventured. "When did this start?"

"Er, this morning I think," said Charm vaguely. Her headache was getting worse. "I was opening my birthday cards after breakfast. Someone sent me some flowers . . . my head started to ache and—"

"What flowers?" enquired the Silversmith suspiciously.

"Those," said Charm. She pointed to the bouquet of dark purple blooms, with their powerful perfume.

The Silversmith caught sight of the card that came with them, and immediately her mystic powers picked up bad vibrations from the handwriting:

To Her Majesty,
Happy Birthday!
from a well-wisher
x x

"Those flowers aren't from a *well-wisher*," said the Silversmith angrily. "They're from ZORGAN!"

156

Without another word, she grabbed the flowers and flung them out of a window. This simple act had an amazing effect on Charm's headache *and* the purple cloud. They instantly disappeared! Charm looked relieved and confused at the same time.

"Zorgan put you under some sort of doubting spell," explained the Silversmith. "No wonder you thought badly of Sesame."

"Poor Sesame!" cried Charm. "That balam⁎ magician tricked me. I wish I could tell Sesame how sorry I am."

"Rashee,"⁎⁎ said the Silversmith soothingly, and gave Charm her bouquet of poppies. "One day you *will* meet Sesame, I promise. There'll come a time when we can explain everything to her. Until then, I know she'll go on looking for your charms."

* *
⁎ Balam — cursed or damned
⁎⁎ Rashee — hush; be still. A word of reassurance

Just then a red-faced, flustered-looking Dork arrived.

"Ahem. Er . . . I regret to inform Your Majesty that I failed to . . . that is . . . I was unable to arrest Sesame Brown because I, er . . . unfortunately tripped over the gatekeeper's tail—"

"Wonderful!" exclaimed Charm, clapping her hands with joy. "Simply wonderful. Sesame Brown is NOT a thief. I was under some . . . misapprehension. Here, Officer Dork. Have a piece of birthday cake!"

Dork rolled his eyes. He was completely baffled. Girls, he thought. They can never make their minds up! But, of course, he said nothing of the sort to the queen, and handed her the scroll, which Pogo the gatekeeper, had given him.

Charm read it with the Silversmith.

"This is a fascinating part of our history," said Charm, her eyes shining with delight. "Thanks to Sesame and her friends, Agapogo's magical silver is no longer a mystery. Three cheers for the Charmseekers!"

Twelve

The Silversmith arrives in her workshop and the first thing she sees are the thirteen magic candles.

"Ah!" she sighs. "Another candle has gone out. It is the silver coin." It is with Sesame, together with the seven charms she has already found. Eight charms safe in her Seeker's care.

"Good," she murmurs. "Thank you, Charmseekers! You have conquered many dangers to find these precious charms, although I fear there are many more challenges to overcome. Have courage to go on with your quest, Sesame!"

Five magic candles glow and each of them will burn until its lost charm is found – no matter how long it takes.

She crosses to the window and looks out into the starry heavens, reflecting on the strange happenings of the day. So, Zorgan *almost* succeeded in turning Charm against Sesame. This was a powerful spell and cunningly planned. Who knows what might have happened if she had not attended Charm's party tonight! And no doubt the wretched magician has more tricks up his sleeve. Her Seeker must beware . . .

What's this? A shooting star! A heavenly beacon of light, streaks across the sky. To where? All the way to Sesame's world? But that is another story. It must be told another day!

For Gwen Millward – with thanks and appreciation

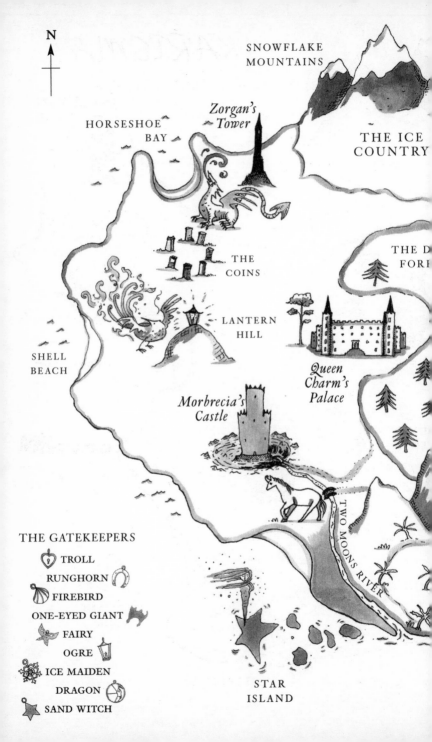

KARISMA

CAPE CAT

CLOVER FIELDS

HEARTMOOR

DOLPHIN BAY

MOUNT TUNA

The Silver Pool

KEY POINT

SWAMPS

JUNGLE

MERMAID ROCK

BUTTERFLY BAY

One

The Silversmith rolls the ancient parchment with care, winds a silver ribbon around it and ties it with a bow.

"A fascinating story," she muses, "and so vividly described by Silvesta.* To think, if it hadn't been for Sesame and her friends this important part of our history may never have been discovered!"

Placing the scroll in a drawer, the Silversmith locks it away. She feels honoured Queen Charm has entrusted her with the historic document.

"Silvesta's story explains everything about the origins of the Silver Pool," she remembers Charm saying. "Since you have charge of the magical silver it's only right you should look after it."

* * * * * * * * * * * * * * * * * * *
*Do you remember Silvesta's story? You can read it in Book Eight: *Secret Treasure*

167

Since then – since Charm's birthday about a mede* ago – she has read the story often, each time gaining more of an insight as to why the Silver Pool is so special. It's unique to Karisma and, of course, the charms she's created from this precious source are special too. Even *she* doesn't fully understand their power. Somehow their positive energy keeps everything in balance; together they keep nature under control – a force for good, protecting the fragile world in their care. As these thoughts race through her head, words from a familiar song dance off her lips:

Thirteen charms on a silver band,
United hold our world in hand . . .
One and all, beware the day
Charms and bracelet break away.
Together they must always stay!

The Silversmith clearly remembers Charm's coronation, when she presented the new queen with her bracelet. Charm knew she held the charms in trust, for the benefit of her people. Trust. Such a small word, thinks the Silversmith, but those who are trusted carry big responsibilities! She recalls

*Mede – month

how Zorgan, the wicked magician, very nearly destroyed Charm's trust in Sesame. She shakes her head at the thought of it and her long, silvery hair falls loosely around her shoulders.

"Thank the stars he didn't succeed!" she exclaims. "Thank goodness Charm knows that one day Sesame will return the lost charms, when she has found them all. Until then, they are safe with her in the Outworld."*

But how safe is her Seeker? Zorgan is in league with the queen's sister, Morbrecia, and his plan to snatch Sesame's locket and put her under a spell, to bring *him* the charms is unthinkable! If only she could find a way to warn Sesame . . .

The Silversmith glances at the thirteen magic candles; five still burn – glowing beacons of hope for their missing charms – and she hopes Sesame will return soon. So far the Charmseekers have outwitted Zorgan and Morbrecia, and Sesame has eight silver charms in her safekeeping.

* *
*Outworld – the name Karismans call our world

Turning to the window,
the Silversmith is amazed to see
a shooting star streaking across the
pale morning sky and, trailing in its wake,
a cascade of sparkling lights.

She sighs. It is a good sign . . .

Two

"How much more can you fit in there?" exclaimed Nic Brown. "It's only a *small* tent."

Sesame squeezed past her dad through the kitchen door, followed by her best friend, Maddy Webb. Each carried armfuls of rugs, sleeping bags, pillows, books, MP3s and teddies.

"Don't worry, Dad," said Sesame, skilfully balancing Alfie on top of her pile. "We'll manage."

"Mm," came Maddy's muffled voice from behind a pillow. "You need loads of stuff for camping, Mr Brown."

Nic shook his head in amusement and watched the girls stagger down the garden path, past the flower beds full of pink and yellow snapdragons, fragrant sweet peas and bright, red poppies to the grassy patch by the apple tree where they'd pitched the tent. It was a warm Saturday afternoon in early summer and he'd agreed Sesame and Maddy could camp overnight.

He was taking Jodie Luck to a glittering awards ceremony in town, but he'd arranged for Sesame's gran, Lossy, to keep an eye on Sesame and Maddy. Leaving the girls to organise themselves, he texted Jodie:

Looking forward to seeing you later. Meet here about 7pm? Nic x

I'll be there. Jodie xx ☺

Sesame lifted the flap and found Chips and Pins already inside the tent. Her inquisitive, mischievous cats couldn't resist exploring.

As soon as she'd unrolled her sleeping-bag Chips settled himself, purring contentedly. Sesame laughed.

"So, you're camping too!" she said.

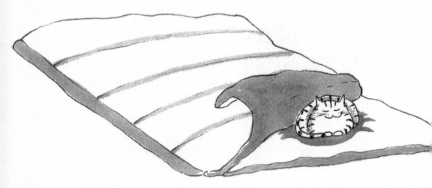

Maddy gave a shout.

"Ouch!"

Pins had pounced on her wiggling toes. Like Sesame, Maddy was wearing shorts and a T-shirt and had been padding around in bare feet. She caught Pins and gave him a cuddle.

"I can't wait for our midnight feast," she said. She produced a bag of jellybeans and offered Sesame some.

"Mm, thanks," said Sesame, taking a handful. "We can tell scary stories in the dark."

"We'll need a torch for spooky faces," said Maddy. She rummaged through her belongings. "Oh, I've forgotten mine."

"I've got one somewhere," said Sesame. "Gran bought me a brill Star-Brite wand torch that glows in the dark. Come on. Race you to the house."

At seven o'clock, Sesame and Maddy were in the kitchen with Lossy, preparing snacks for their midnight feast. Suddenly, Nic appeared in the doorway looking flustered. He was wearing a smart, black dinner jacket with a white shirt, but from his collar dangled a loose bow tie.

"I can't tie this stupid thing," he grumbled. "Not used to dressing up. A lot of fuss if you ask me."

Lossy wiped her hands on her apron and came to his rescue.

"Here, let me do it," she said.

Fascinated, Sesame and Maddy watched her loop the shaped ends of the bow tie over, under, across and through each other, until she'd tied them perfectly. Nic turned to the girls for approval.

"There. How do I look?"

"Cooool!" they drawled.

"You look great, Dad," added Sesame. "Hope you win tonight."

"Win what?" asked Maddy.

Nic looked embarrassed.

"Oh, some award I've been nominated for," he muttered.

"*Some* award!" exploded Sesame. "Er, I think you mean The Daily Times Photojournalist of the Year Award."

"Wow!" said Maddy.

Nic blushed, checked his watch, then patted his pocket.

"Oops, nearly forgot the invitations," he said. "Where *did* I put them?"

Sesame rolled her eyes.

"Here, Dad," she said, handing him two gilt-edged cards from a shelf-tidy, crammed with bills and papers.

Seconds later, the doorbell rang.

"That'll be Jodie," said Nic, and he hurried away to greet her.

The girls gasped with delight when they saw Jodie. Their riding teacher was looking very glamorous in a long, silky, peach dress and high-heeled silver sandals. In one hand she clutched a beaded evening bag, and her earrings sparkled like stars. Nic thought she looked stunning.

"I *love* your dress," said Sesame.

"Gorgeous bag," added Maddy.

"You look lovely," said Lossy, echoing everyone's thoughts.

"Thank you," said Jodie shyly. She turned to Sesame and Maddy. "I hear you two are camping tonight. What fun!"

Nic glanced at his watch again.

"Time to go."

Lossy and the girls went to the car, to see them off.

"Good luck!" everyone chorused, as Nic and Jodie drove away.

Shortly afterwards, Sesame and Maddy made their way to the tent. It was a clear, starry night and the moon was full. Sesame had found her torch, but she didn't switch it on – the garden was flooded with moonlight. They heard Lossy call to them from the back door:

"I'll be down soon to say goodnight, girls."

Sesame waved and Lossy went inside. She switched on the television and settled down to watch the news.

Meanwhile, the girls were crossing the lawn when Sesame's necklace began to tingle. She'd felt this tingling sensation many times before, as though her special locket was trying to tell her something. Goose pimples pricked the nape of her neck and her tummy fluttered with excitement. What could it mean this time?

Something made her look up and she stopped dead in her tracks. Maddy crashed into her. She'd been carrying a plate of sandwiches and midnight treats which went flying.

"Ses," she protested. "You might've warned me—"

"Look," said Sesame. "A shooting star!"

"Wicked!" Maddy exclaimed.

They gawped in wonder at the meteor, which was sprinkling a trail of tiny stars across the heavens. Without warning, they found themselves caught up in the whirl of its glittering, golden light, twirling them faster and faster until Sesame felt her feet leave the ground.

"Help!" she cried, flinging out her arms to steady herself.

"Wait for me!" yelled Maddy.

Just in time she grabbed Sesame's foot and held on tight. Together they rocketed skywards, scarcely able to breathe they were going so fast. It was like zooming up in a lift – fifty floors without stopping – hurtling through time and space, in the wake of the star. Without a doubt, the Charmseekers knew they were on their way to the magical world of Karisma.

Three

Sesame and Maddy travelled from darkness to daylight in no time. Soon they were descending through a cascade of gold pinpricks of light, until they landed *Thump! Bump!* on a sandy beach. Sesame shook herself, amazed to find she was still holding her torch. She put it in the pocket of her shorts and looked about. Maddy lay sprawled nearby. She moaned as she got to her feet.

"Ow," she said, rubbing her knee. "Where are we?"

"Not sure . . ." said Sesame slowly. "It looks a *bit* like Butterfly Bay but—" She could see a headland jutting into the sea and beyond that, a distant shore. "I think we're on an island."

They were still wondering where they were when a blast of wind got up, so fierce it nearly blew them over. A spinning, spiralling golden cloud whirled from the sand, and from it emerged the figure of a woman.

She had a shawl of bright green seaweed fronds draped about her shoulders, her tangled hair was plaited with seashells.

"Fairday,* Charmseekers. I'm Ramora, Gatekeeper Nine. Welcome to Star Island!"

* *
*Fairday – a typical Karisman friendly greeting

For a few seconds the girls stared at her in stunned amazement, before Sesame managed to say:

"Hi! I'm— "

"Sesame Brown," said Ramora. "I know all about you and your friend, Maddy Webb. It's all in the weeds. I read them, you see."

Maddy looked puzzled.

"Weeds?"

"I'll show you," said Ramora. "Come in."

"In where?" asked Sesame. She couldn't see a building anywhere.

Ramora clapped her hands. There was a

BANG! A mini sand storm, then **POOF!**

A wooden hut appeared.

"My place," said Ramora.

"Um, excuse me," said Sesame, following Ramora into her hut. "Are you a . . . witch?"

"Not *a* witch," replied Ramora indignantly. "A *sand* witch."

Maddy started to giggle. The vision of a sandwich on a broomstick entered her head, but she didn't think Ramora would find it funny. She swallowed hard to control herself and followed Sesame inside.

Together they stepped into a cosy sitting room lit by lamps with pearly lampshades. A driftwood fire burned brightly in the fireplace. The room was crammed with curious things;

pots, bowls, trinkets and knick-knacks littered every shelf and table; on the walls were sea charts, star maps and pictures. A picture of the thirteen magical charms immediately caught Sesame's eye.

She pointed out five of them to the gatekeeper.

"The moon, star, dolphin, cloverleaf and key are still missing," she explained. "We've come to look for them. Sesame Brown will track them down!"

"We've found all the others," said Maddy.

"Yes, I know," said Ramora, with a smile. "The weeds, remember?" She took a clump of fresh seaweed from a jar and spread the strands on a tray. "They tell tales, if you know how to read them."

"Can we have a go?" asked Maddy.

"Please do," said Ramora.

Maddy and Sesame studied the seaweed for a short while. Maddy gave up, disappointed because she couldn't see a thing. But Sesame thought she'd spotted something.

"Look," she said, "A little star!"

"You have the gift of a Seeker," Ramora murmured. "The charm must be here somewhere . . . *so*, keep your eyes and ears open. The sooner you find *all* the charms the better! That evil magician Zorgan is after them." Catching sight of Sesame's necklace, she added: "He wants your pretty locket too."

Ramora had only confirmed what Sesame already knew, but hearing the sand witch say it sent shivers down her spine.

"Why *does* Zorgan want my locket?" she asked.

"Ah," said Ramora, pausing to choose her words carefully. Although she didn't want to scare Sesame, she had to warn her about the magician. "Zorgan needs a precious belonging, something you treasure. Once he has it he can cast a spell on you. Under his spell, you'd be forced to bring him the charms, even the ones you hold in the Outworld."

"Oh, Ses!" cried Maddy.

Although it was worse than she'd feared, Sesame wasn't put off. In fact, she felt more determined than ever to complete her quest.

"Don't worry," she said. "There's no way I'd give Zorgan the charms. They belong to Queen Charm!"

Ramora chuckled.

"That's the spirit," she said, and peered into her seaweed. Something she saw in the weeds made her frown. "Hushish!"* she exclaimed. "Bad sign. I see the letter 'M'."

Sesame and Maddy looked at each other.

"Morbrecia!" they groaned.

"I'm afraid so," said Ramora. "She'll make trouble for you. Morbrecia and Zorgan – they're in this together."

"Let's go, Maddy," said Sesame. "We must find the charm before Morbrecia does."

When they were all standing outside the hut, Maddy remembered about the gate.

"What time do we have to be back?" she asked Ramora.

* *
*Hushish – a word used to express dismay

"Look for my chimney," said the gatekeeper. "Six puffs of smoke and the gate shuts."

Then she went inside and closed the door.

Four

Morbrecia's favourite magical doll, Elmo, sat watching Morbrecia stick pins into Sesame's shoe! How fortunate for Sesame, thought Elmo, that she isn't wearing it! Not that it mattered. Sesame would soon feel the power of the pins, wherever she was . . .

The item of footwear under attack was a flip-flop – the one Sesame had lost on Agapogo Day a few medes ago. Morbrecia recalled she'd been chasing Sesame Brown and Maddy Webb through the streets of Lantern Hill. Sesame had found the beautiful silver shell and Morbrecia had *so* nearly snatched it from her. She jabbed yet another pin into the sandal and turned to Elmo.

"Sesame escaped and all I got was her shoe!" she said bitterly. "So far she's been lucky. She's got away with eight charms. But next time I'll be ready for her—"

Morbrecia stopped. Elmo's lips had started to move and suddenly words came tumbling from her mouth. Morbrecia knew they were not Elmo's words, not her voice. She'd know that voice anywhere. Zorgan! He used Elmo as a way to communicate with Morbrecia, so they could plot and plan together.

"Put aside the Seeker's shoe,
There's more important work to do.
Star Island is the place to be,
To lie in wait for - S-e-s-a-m-e!"

"I'll go to Star Island at once," said Morbrecia eagerly, although she grimaced at the idea of a boat trip. She felt seasick just thinking about it.

Five

The Charmseekers struck out along the bay and climbed the headland Sesame had seen earlier. From here they could see the whole of Star Island; it was shaped like a five pointed star. When they looked across the turquoise sea towards the mainland of Karisma, they picked out the familiar shape of Morbrecia's castle. With a sinking feeling, they realised it wasn't far away.

"I hope Morbrecia hasn't spotted us," said Maddy anxiously.

Sesame hoped so too. If the star charm *was* here, they'd have to work fast, before she caught up with them. But where should they begin? Sesame fingered her locket, trying to decide, but she couldn't get Ramora's warning about Zorgan out of her head. Forewarned, she'd have to take extra care of her locket from now on. Suddenly she felt it tingle as she looked towards a long, sandy beach bordered by cliffs, and she was sure this was a sign.

"Come on," she said to Maddy. "We'll start there."

The tide was out. Sesame and Maddy walked barefoot along a stretch of golden sand, peering into rock pools and under stones, hoping to catch a tell tale glint of silver. Splashing through a shallow pool, Sesame felt a sharp pain in her left foot. It was quickly followed by another and another. It was like pins and needles, only worse.

"Ouch!" she yelped, hopping on one leg.

"What's up, Ses?" said Maddy.

"I must have trodden on something," said Sesame.

They hunted round for a sharp object, but there was nothing there. Sesame gave her sore foot a rub.

"Weird," she said. And thought no more of it.

Some time later, as they rounded a craggy cliff, they were surprised to see footprints in the sand. Large, webbed footprints . . . and lots of them.

"I wonder who they belong to?" said Sesame, scanning the beach. She couldn't see anyone about.

"Big ducks?" joked Maddy.

"Ssh!" said Sesame. "Listen."

It was the unmistakable sound of voices singing:

"Pebbles, shells, glass and wood,
Shiny metal findings.
We're the folk who pick them up –
The lost and left-behindings!"

When the singers came marching out from behind a big rock, Sesame and Maddy found themselves gawping at five skinny boys. They had slime-green bodies and flat, webbed feet and each carried a bulging sack.

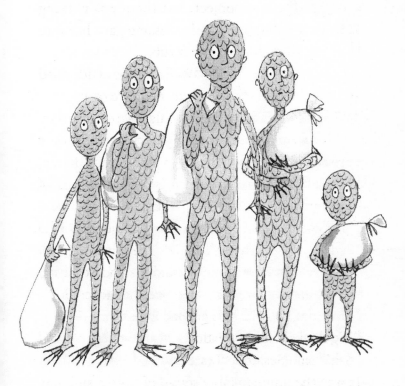

The boys stopped singing and looked very alarmed to see strangers on their beach. The biggest took a step forward and eyed the girls suspiciously.

"Who are you?" he said.

"I'm Sesame," said Sesame. "This is my friend Maddy. Who are *you*?"

"Tyke," said Tyke. "We're Urchins."* He jabbed a thumb at his companions. "My chinners."**

His friends called out their names:

"I'm Gumba! Lumsy! Lug! Fiz!"

"Do you live on Star Island?" asked Maddy.

Tyke shuffled his webbed feet and avoided answering her question.

"We're . . . *staying* here," he said.

"We're from The Swamps," said Gumba, with a nod towards the mainland.

"I think we've been there!" said Sesame. She remembered the time she, Maddy, Gemma and Liz had come to Karisma in a magic bubble. They'd landed in a marshy place and had to squelch through the mud in their slippers. Maybe *that's* why urchins have webbed feet, she thought.

"How did you get here?" Maddy asked.

"We were fishing off rocks near Butterfly Bay," said Lumsy. He looked embarrassed: "Got cut off by the tide . . ."

"Clung to some driftwood," added Lug, "and landed here."

* *

*Urchins – web-footed people of The Swamps

**Chinners – Urchin slang, meaning 'mates'

196

The smallest urchin called Fiz began to sniffle.

"I want to go home," he said.

"Well, you can't," shouted Tyke. "We're stuck!"

There was an awkward silence. Sesame and Maddy felt especially sorry for Fiz, but they couldn't see how they could help. Maddy tried to make conversation.

"We're Charmseekers—" she began.

"Charm-s-e-e-k-e-r-s," drawled Tyke. "You're looking for charms?"

"You won't find anything here," said Gumba. "It's boring. We've found all there is to find."

"Anyway this is *our* beach now," said Lumsy defensively. "Everything belongs to us."

"They're our left-behindings," said Lug.

"Left-behindings?" queried Maddy.

Tyke rattled the contents of his sack.

"Ah," said Sesame, cottoning on. She remembered their song: 'Pebbles, shells, glass and wood, shiny metal findings . . .' "You *collect* things!" As she said it, an idea whizzed into her head. Perhaps the urchins could help them look for the charm? There was a chance they'd already found it. She was wondering how best to ask them, when Maddy blurted out:

"We collect charms!"

Sesame rolled her eyes at Maddy. The urchins – all except Fiz – didn't look too happy. Fiz thought the girls seemed friendly, so he smiled at them shyly.

"Um, not exactly," said Sesame, thinking fast. "We're searching for some lost charms so we can give them back to Queen Charm."

"One of them *might* be on the island," said Maddy. "A silver star. Have you seen it?"

"No!" said Lumsy, a little too quickly.

Fiz shot him a look.

"Lumsy—" he began.

But the other urchins glared at him and Fiz cowered, afraid to say  more. Sesame felt sure they knew *something* about the charm and the thought of them not telling her made her mad.

Losing your temper isn't going to help, she told herself. Keep your cool, Sesame. Try and gain their trust . . .

"*Please* help us," she said. "It's really important we find the charms. They're magic. I don't know how, but they help nature, the weather, the climate – *everything*. Since they were stolen from the queen, terrible things have been happening. The winds have changed, butterflies can't migrate, the ice is melting, crops have been ruined . . . oh, loads of stuff!"

"Yes," said Maddy. "And things will go on getting worse, until all the charms are found."

"Is that why we got cut off by the tide?" asked Fiz timidly. "Was it because the magic charms were lost?"

His four friends sniggered. To the girls' dismay, none of what they'd said seemed to have had the slightest effect on *them*. Tyke folded his arms and scowled at Sesame.

"Why should we believe you?" he said. "I bet you're making it up. Nothing bad's happened here. We're jammo." *

"You just want our left-behindings," said Gumba.

"We *might* know where the charm is . . ." teased Lumsy.

* *
✶ Jammo – Urchin slang for good or okay

"Even if we did, we wouldn't tell you!" said Lug.

And they ran off singing, tugging a reluctant Fiz along with them.

"Pebbles, shells, glass
and wood, shiny metal findings.
We're the folk who pick them up
- the lost and left- behindings!"

Six

"Stop rocking the boat," yelled Morbrecia. "I feel sick!"

After Zorgan's tip about Sesame's whereabouts, Morbrecia had hastily picked four footmen and ordered them to sail her to Star Island. A brisk breeze whipped up the waves. The footmen did their best to handle the billowing sails, but it seemed the wind was blowing them on a course of its own. And her crew had never sailed before. Miserably, Morbrecia hung over the side, her face an astonishing shade of green. And still the sea swelled up and down, up and down . . .

At last, they reached Star Island. The crew anchored off a sandy cove and Morbrecia waded ashore. Relieved to be on dry land, she ran quickly across the sand and hid behind a rock. In her haste, as she tripped and scrambled over the hot sand, a silver buckle flew off her shoe.

"Blatz!"* she cursed. She could see the buckle lying a little way away, but she didn't want to be seen. "I'll fetch it later," she said.

She scanned the beach. To her right was a maze of rocks and to her left, five small caves at the foot of a cliff. She could see no sign of Sesame. Was the Charmseeker alone or with friends? Zorgan hadn't said. She wished she could look into his crystal ball and see what was going on . . .

****

*Blatz – a really angry exclamation

Zorgan, meanwhile, had been keeping his eye on Sesame and Maddy. Ever since they'd arrived on Star Island, he'd observed their every move through his crystal ball. He'd even glimpsed inside Ramora's hut, while she was reading her seaweed. He'd been very surprised to learn the gatekeeper knew of his plans to put a spell on Sesame . . .

"Interfering witch and her weeds!" he fumed. "Ramora knows too much for her own good. But I *will* have Sesame's locket. She *will* bring me the charms!"

From his Star Room, Zorgan looked across to the island. He prided himself on having taken control of Morbrecia's boat, setting it on course for one particular beach. He smiled, as he stroked his pet bandrall,✴ Vanda.

"My windy spell did the trick," he told her with

✴ ✴

✴ **Bandrall** – rare flying mammal, native to Karisma

smug satisfaction. "Now it's up to Morbrecia. She must deal with Sesame Brown!"

"One of them must have found the charm," said Sesame crossly. "I *know* it."

Maddy agreed.

"It was the way they looked at each other," she said. "I wonder who?"

"Even if we knew," said Sesame, "how would we persuade him to give it up? I bet if Fiz had found the star he'd have said, but he's afraid of the others. They're SO mean to him."

"Mm," commiserated Maddy. "And they don't care about what's happening in Karisma. Just because they're okay, they think nothing else matters. They can't be bothered to help."

"I reckon they're just bored," said Sesame. "They're collecting 'lost and left-behindings' because there's nothing else to do."

"In a way that's good, isn't it?" said Maddy.

"Yes, it's brill," agreed Sesame. "The urchins don't know it, but they're helping the environment!"

"I wonder what they're going to do with all that stuff?" said Maddy. "I haven't noticed any recycling banks here."

Sesame grinned.

"Well, maybe they could start one!" she said.

They'd been following the urchins' footprints through a maze of rocks and had come to a sandy cove. Anchored a little way off shore they saw a sailing boat.

"I wonder who that belongs to?" said Maddy. "I can't see anyone about."

The girls were still puzzling over the boat and where the urchins could have gone, when they spotted the five caves.

"I reckon they're hiding in there," said Sesame.

"And one of them has the charm!" said Maddy.

She felt so cross and frustrated with the urchins that she walked round in circles, kicking at the sand. Sesame leaned against a rock to think.

"The urchins are a problem," she said, "but we've faced more difficult challenges than them. Remember the gribblers⁎ and the skreels?" ⁎ ⁎

⁎ **Gribbler** — extremely unpleasant goblin-like creature with yellow teeth and bad breath
⁎⁎ **Skreel** — small flesh-eating fish

Maddy nodded and came over.

"And Zorgan's pixies, Nix and Dina," she said.

"Not forgetting the drakons!"* added Sesame.

"So what now?" said Maddy. "We haven't got time to play stupid guessing games with the urchins. It won't be long before the gate closes."

"I know," said Sesame. "But we can't give up. Anyway I've just thought of a brilliant plan . . ."

* *
*Drakon – large fire-breathing insect

Seven

"We're going to trick them into *showing* us!" said Sesame.

"R-i-g-h-t," said Maddy.

Sesame explained.

"Look, we know they pick things up from the beach," she said. "Remember their song? Well, supposing they each collect one type of thing. Fiz was about to tell us before the others shut him up. Maybe Tyke likes pebbles; Gumba, shells; Fiz, glass . . . get it? That means one of them collects *shiny metal*—"

"Cool!" said Maddy. "So one of them'll have the

 charm. But I don't see how they're going to show us. "

"You soon will," said Sesame. "Listen. Here's what we'll do . . ."

When she'd finished, they gave each other their secret Charmseekers hand sign, for luck.

208

Meanwhile, from her hiding place behind a craggy rock, Morbrecia had a perfect view of the girls. At first, it seemed the pair were busily occupied looking for the charms. Morbrecia chuckled to herself. With any luck those interfering Charmseekers will find a charm, she thought. And I'll be waiting to grab it! However, after a while, Morbrecia had the feeling something wasn't quite right. She was baffled. What *were* they up to?

"Ooo! Here's a pretty shell," exclaimed Sesame, in a loud voice. She was holding up an empty shell, pearly-pink with bright red stripes.

"Look, Ses," cried Maddy. "I've found some driftwood and a pebble!"

They were shouting on purpose, hoping to attract the urchins' attention. It was all part of Sesame's plan. After they'd been searching for a bit longer, Maddy said out of the corner of her mouth:

"Supposing we don't find any glass and metal things?"

"We must," said Sesame. "My idea won't work without them."

They both knew time was slipping by. They'd been keeping an eye on Ramora's hut on the far side of the cove; the last time Maddy checked, she'd counted three puffs of smoke from the chimney.

Maddy suddenly let out an excited squeal. She'd spotted a broken necklace of glass beads, washed up on the shore. She held it up, hoping the urchins might see. A few minutes later, Sesame chanced upon something silver, glinting in the sand. Her tummy flipped and, for a thrilling moment, she thought she'd found a charm. To her disappointment, she discovered it was only a shiny shoe buckle.

"You should be pleased," said Maddy. "Now we can set the trap!"

The girls strolled near the caves, casually dropping the shell, pebble, driftwood, necklace and buckle as they went along.

Sesame and Maddy wandered about, as if they had all the time in the world to enjoy themselves. Sesame dramatically wiped her hand across her forehead.

"Phew! I'm really hot," she shouted. "Let's go for a swim!"

"Good idea," cried Maddy. "The sea looks lovely."

But instead of swimming, they hid behind some rocks and watched to see what would happen. They didn't have to wait long. The urchins couldn't resist the 'left-behindings'. They came scuttling out of their caves and each put something in his sack . . .

Can you see what each urchin put in his sack? Remember, only one of them collects shiny metal things, so who is most likely to have the charm? Is it Tyke, Gumba, Lumsy, Lug or Fiz?

Sesame's plan was working! First came Tyke . . . then Gumba . . . Lug was next . . . followed by Fiz . . . And last of all came Lumsy, who picked up the shiny silver buckle! He was about to put it in his sack, when Sesame and Maddy sprang from their hiding place.

"You're the one with the charm!" accused Sesame.

"Open your sack," demanded Maddy.

Taken by surprise, Lumsy dropped the buckle. But he soon recovered.

"What if I have?" he sneered. "What are you going to do about it?"

Sesame was ready. She smiled sweetly at him.

"Swap you for it?" she said.

"Swap what?" said Lumsy. His friends crowded round, curious to see what Sesame had to offer.

"This," she said, suddenly producing her torch. "My glow-in-the-dark Star-Brite wand torch! Guaranteed waterproof and shockproof." She switched it on and off, for dramatic effect.

The urchins were awestruck. They thought the torch was amazing.

"A light stick!" said Tyke, taking a step closer.

"It must be magic," said Gumba.

"Mm," said Maddy, trying to keep a straight face.

"You can use it in emergencies," added Sesame.

She switched her Star-Brite wand torch to signal mode and set off a flashing beacon.

"Done!" cried Lumsy.

He grabbed the torch, then shook the contents from his sack. A jumbled assortment of tins, a rusty bucket, a bent spoon, a broken watch, a length of chain, an iron ring and some coins came spilling out. Frantically, Sesame and Maddy sorted through the junk, but they couldn't see the charm.

"Where is it?" cried Sesame, afraid the urchin had tricked her.

"I-I-haven't got it," said Lumsy, snatching up his sack. "Fooled you though, didn't I!"

"Give it to me," said Sesame. making a grab for the sack. "I want to see for myself."

But Lumsy was too quick and backed away.

"You'll have to catch me first," he said.

"Oh, Lumsy!" cried Fiz. "That's not fair."

The other urchins rounded on him, but this time he stood up to them.

215

"I think we should help the Charmseekers," said Fiz, sounding much bolder than he felt. "It's important they find all the magical charms 'cos they help everything and I know you've got the star Lumsy 'cos I saw you pick it up!"

Lumsy was furious. He made to give Fiz a cuff round the ear, but Tyke stopped him. He'd been thinking. What if the star charm was magic, as Sesame had said it was. If they kept it, would it bring them bad luck? Tyke took charge of the situation.

"Open the sack," he ordered Lumsy.

"Wha—" began Lumsy.

"Just do it," said Tyke.

Lumsy didn't dare argue with Tyke. Moodily he opened his sack and gave it another shake and . . . out flew the little star! It was perfect. The silver charm twinkled and shone with a shimmering light of its own – as bright as any star in the sky.

Sesame and Maddy were never quite sure what happened next. Everything whizzed by in a blur. All they could remember was Morbrecia appearing from nowhere to snatch the charm.

It was the moment the princess had been waiting for. Lurking behind her rock, watching and listening, she'd timed her attack perfectly. The second after Morbrecia saw the star fall from Lumsy's sack, she sprang into action. She raced from her hiding place, her jet-black hair streaming in the wind.

"Mine!" she screeched, as she swooped on the charm.

Instinctively, Sesame dived for the star. Maddy made a grab for Morbrecia's shoe — the one without the buckle — and it slipped off her foot.

Morbrecia aimed a swift kick at Maddy, and missed. Sesame, meanwhile, was fiercely struggling to release the charm from Morbrecia's clamped fist.

"LET GO!" she cried, but as she fought, her locket got caught in Morbrecia's hair.

"Ow!" yelped Morbrecia, using her free hand to wrench the locket from her locks. She used *such* force that – *SNAP!* The chain broke. Seizing her chance, Morbrecia snatched the locket from Sesame's neck and held it up triumphantly.

"Oh!" wailed Sesame.

"No!" shouted Maddy.

"Vixee!"* exclaimed Morbrecia. "A charm *and* your locket, Sesame Brown. You're in BIG trouble now!"

Sesame lunged at her, but Morbrecia was too quick. She ran, one shoe on and the other off, with Sesame and Maddy pelting after her.

* * * * * * * * * * * * * * *

* **Vixee** – a gleeful, triumphant exclamation meaning great or wicked

218

During this time, the urchins had been oblivious to everything going on around them – all except Fiz, who had stood aside, watching with a bewildered expression on his face. He was too little to help Sesame and Maddy wrestle the charm from Morbrecia and, to make matters worse, a fight had broken out between the urchins.

After Lumsy had taken possession of Sesame's torch, Tyke, Gumba and Lug quarrelled over it. First Tyke snatched it from Lumsy, then Gumba grabbed it from Tyke, who was jumped on by Lug. By the time they'd all stopped fighting and had agreed to share the torch, Sesame and Maddy were nowhere in sight. But Fiz had watched them go . . .

★ ⭒ ★

Zorgan could barely contain his excitement. He'd been following Morbrecia's progress in his crystal ball, and had seen her swoop on the charm *and* snatch Sesame's locket.

"Spallah!"★ he exclaimed. "I shall soon have Sesame under my spell."

He was also aware that time was running out for the Charmseekers to return to the gate. Zorgan crossed the room to look through his powerful

* *
★ Spallah – excellent! A triumphant expression

telescope. He swivelled the eyepiece and focused it on the gatekeeper's hut. Between the hut and the cove was a rocky bay. Sesame mustn't get away. Somehow he must cut off her escape . . .

The magician opened his Book of Tried and Trusted Sea Spells and leafed through the pages, until he found one that sounded just right. For maximum effect, the spell required him to drink some salty water, before chanting the words.

Nix and Dina were standing by. Zorgan turned to the pixies, barking orders.

"Bring me water, a large goblet and some salt," he commanded.

Immediately the pixies flew off to carry out their tasks. Nix returned first, struggling with the biggest goblet she could find. Then came Dina with a jug of water and a pot of salt. Zorgan poured the water into the goblet, added the salt and swirled it around. He held his nose, took a sip and . . . SPAT IT OUT. It tasted foul!

He was sure the spell would work anyway, so he tipped the salty drink away and intoned:

"Ebb and flow, come and go,
Waves high, waters low.
Tide turn, oh, salty sea –
Seal the fate of S-e-s-a-m-e!"

Back on the beach Sesame and Maddy were gaining on Morbrecia. Hampered by losing her shoe, Morbrecia couldn't run as quickly as the girls. Cursing Maddy, she splashed through a rock pool and didn't see the crab . . .

It was huge – a giant of a beast – waving two enormous pincers and lying in wait for its prey. When Morbrecia's bare foot landed right in front of it –

SNAP!

The crab clamped her toe in one colossal claw.

"OWWOOO!"

screamed Morbrecia, letting fly Sesame's locket and the charm in one go.

The Charmseekers couldn't believe their luck. The locket went sailing through the air and Maddy, who was a few steps ahead of Sesame, caught it neatly. Morbrecia looked daggers at Maddy, but there was nothing she could do. The crab clung on tight and she couldn't move. The star charm spiralled and fell *smack* into the crab's other claw!

"This is so not fair!" wailed Sesame, in frustration. One second the charm had been flying free. Then it wasn't.

But what happened next took them all by surprise. The tide turned without warning and, with a thunderous roar, a terrifying wall of water rose from the sea. Morbrecia and the girls stared in horror. It was the biggest wave they had ever seen – and it was heading straight for them!

Nine

Morbrecia was terrified. She screamed at her footmen in the boat; they had been lying on deck having a nap.

"Don't just sit there, magworts.* Help me!"

Maddy looked panic-stricken and wanted to run. Sesame was scared stiff too. She glanced at the wall of water thundering towards them. In a few minutes, she reckoned, it would swamp them. Out of the corner of her eye, she spotted five small boys pelting towards them, carrying their sacks of left-behindings. The urchins had seen the wave coming and hoped the Charmseekers could help. Fiz was leading the way, waving Sesame's torch. It was flashing a bright orange signal . . .

Meanwhile, Sesame's thoughts were racing.

"We can't leave Morbrecia," she shouted to Maddy. "She'll drown! And there's the charm—"

* *

Magwort — probably the worst name you could call anyone! General term for a fool

224

Without another thought, Sesame tried to prize the giant claw open, to free Morbrecia's foot. Morbrecia looked at Sesame. She could scarcely believe what was happening.

"Why—?" she began then yelped with pain. "Ouch! That hurt. Watch what you're doing!"

Taking no notice, Sesame strained with all her strength, until suddenly the claw snapped open, and Morbrecia was free. Cursing the crab and without a backwards glance, she limped away to her boat.

The crab fixed Sesame with two, tiny black eyes. In a split-second, there passed between them some kind of mutual trust and understanding. Somehow the crab knew Sesame had come to help, knew she should have care of the charm. And with a *click!* she released the star.

225

"At last!" said Sesame, clasping it in her hand. Next instant, she and Maddy were swept off the rocks, along with the five urchins – everyone buoyed along on the crest of a foaming wave. Maddy screamed and grabbed Sesame's hand.

"Wha-what's happening?" she yelled.

They were all skimming along on the wave like surfers and going so fast it took their breath away.

"**Weeeeee!**"

shouted Tyke, Gumba, Lumsy, Lug and Fiz. It was all they could do to hold on to their sacks.

"Look!" shouted Sesame, pointing ahead. She could see Ramora's hut and puffs of smoke from the chimney. "The wave is taking us to the gate!"

The sand witch was waiting for them as the wave gently dumped the girls at her feet. Ramora clapped her hands and shooed it back to sea.

"Take the urchins safely home," Ramora whispered to the wave, then she added with a mysterious smile, "Thank you."

After the urchins had waved and shouted their goodbyes and thank you's to the Charmseekers, Sesame turned to Ramora.

"We've got the charm," she said. Proudly, she showed the gatekeeper the little star.

"Morbrecia nearly got away with Sesame's locket!" gasped Maddy. She was still holding tight to the broken chain.

"I know," said Ramora. "I saw it in the weeds. I hope Morbrecia appreciates your kindness, Sesame, though I doubt it! Now hurry, Charmseekers. The gate is closing. Setfair.* Come back soon!"

* *
*Setfair – goodbye and good luck

Sesame and Maddy ran into a gold and silvery, slightly gritty, mist that was rising from the sand. It spun them round, faster and faster, until they were spinning through the air, flying through the pink clouds of sunset, into the starry, night sky of home.

They drifted down on a beam of moonlight and landed on the lawn. Chips and Pins greeted them, purring. After their amazing adventure, the girls were in a daze and it took them a few minutes to recover. Everything was exactly as they'd left it – except for some tell tale grains of sand sprinkled on their sleeping bags.

Soon they heard Lossy calling their names, as she came down the garden path.

"Sleeping bags, quick!" whispered Sesame, groping around in the dark. "I wish I had my torch!"

"I wonder if those urchins have still got it," said Maddy, unzipping her bag.

When Lossy lifted the flap, a shaft of moonlight shone on the girls' smiling faces.

"Everything all right, campers?" she asked.

"We're fine, Gran," said Sesame happily.

"Yes," said Maddy. "Camping is cool."

"Good," said Lossy. "Don't stay up too late talking. I know what you two are like!"

"I hope Dad wins the award tonight," said Sesame, kissing her gran goodnight.

"I have a sneaking feeling he might," said Lossy.

And she went back to the house.

☆　　☆　　☆　　☆

Sesame had thought to slip her special jewellery box under her pillow. Now, by the light of the moon, she opened it. She and Maddy took it in turns to hold the silver star charm, turning it this way and that to admire the way it glistened, before Sesame carefully placed it with the others in the box. Seeing the nine beautiful charms together, remembering all they'd been through to find them, gave the girls a thrill.

"Gosh," said Maddy. "I hope we find the others before Zorgan and Morbrecia do." She gave a sleepy yawn. "D'you think we will, Ses?"

"We must," said Sesame, firmly closing the lid. "Whatever it takes . . ."

Sesame looked at her broken necklace. A little shiver ran down her spine, as she remembered how savagely Morbrecia had wrenched it from her. She'd come SO close to losing it! The locket, she knew, was easily mended. Keeping it safe from Zorgan was the problem.

The moon slipped behind a cloud, as Sesame zipped up the tent. Later, when Lossy peeped in to make sure all was well, she found the girls sound asleep.

Ten

The Silversmith claps her hands with joy. Sesame has the little star charm safe! The magic candle that bears its name has gone out. Now four candles remain alight – four charms yet to be found. She remembers each one so clearly; the crescent-moon, the cloverleaf, the key and the dolphin . . .

She knows the Charmseekers have put themselves at risk to save the star charm. And this time something happened to make her fear more than ever for her Seeker. She knew the instant Sesame had been parted from her locket. She'd felt the pain of it breaking. It was as if something had snapped inside her. For a while, she'd felt their bond broken, and had known that her Seeker was in grave danger of falling under Zorgan's spell. But all is well, she tells herself, for the time being at least . . .

The Silversmith knows she has chosen wisely in trusting Sesame to complete her quest. Her Seeker cares for her own world and for Karisma, too. She won't give up until she's found all the charms. Meanwhile, Karisma is in peril and nowhere has escaped the consequences of Zorgan's foolishness in scattering the charms. Neither on land, nor in the air, nor in the sea. Even in the depths of the ocean, things have been thrown out of balance and the mermaids and sea creatures are suffering . . . but that is another story. It must be told another day!

Acknowledgements

I owe a debt of gratitude to all those who have worked behind the scenes at Orion Children's Books and beyond to bring the *Charmseekers* books and their thirteen delightful charms to you. Since it would take more space than this edition allows to mention individuals by name, suffice it to say that I'm hugely grateful to my publishers and everyone involved with the publication of this series. In particular, my special thanks go to: my publisher, Fiona Kennedy, for her creative and skilful editing; my agent, Rosemary Sandberg; Jenny Glencross and Jane Hughes (Editorial); Alex Nicholas and Helen Speedy (Rights) Loulou Clark and Helen Ewing (Design); Clare Hennessy (Production); Jessica Killingley and Jo Dawson (Marketing); Pandora White (Orion Audio Books); Imogen Adams (Website designer – www.hammerinheels.com); Neil Pymer, the real Spinner Shindigs, for kind permission to use his name; and last, but by no means least, a million thanks go to my husband Tom for his inexhaustible patience, critical appraisal and support along the way.

Amy Tree

Join me, Sesame Brown, in the magical
world of Karisma — and you can be
a Charmseeker too!

For more about the books, regular
Charmseeker updates, fun and games,
and everything you ever wanted to know
about Sesame Brown and her friends,

www.Charmseekers.co.uk

Join the Charmseekers

at

www.Charmseekers.co.uk

Join the Charmseekers

at

www.Charmseekers.co.uk